THE DELIVERANCE OF SANCTUARY

IKHTISAD AHMED

authorHOUSE®

AuthorHouse™ UK Ltd.
500 Avebury Boulevard
Central Milton Keynes, MK9 2BE
www.authorhouse.co.uk
Phone: 08001974150

© 2010 Ikhtisad Ahmed. All rights reserved.

No part of this book may be reproduced, stored in a retrieval system, or transmitted by any means without the written permission of the author.

First published by AuthorHouse 5/28/2010

ISBN: 978-1-4490-9022-7 (sc)

"Cover designed © Beatrice Wirsén. All rights reserved."

This book is printed on acid-free paper.

To Beatrice Wirsen

my wife, my best friend,
my muse, my inspiration,
my rock, my eternal support,
my love, forever and an eternity

Prologue

Literature is one my greatest loves and passions. My interest in it has made me an ardent student of it, one who aspires to attain some degree of credibility and accomplishment in the field. Existentialism and the Theatre of the Absurd have always enthralled me. Indeed, if I had to pick, I would say that they constitute my favourite and favoured genre. *The Deliverance of Sanctuary* is my homage to the same, a tribute from a pupil taking his first steps into new territory that he hopes to someday master. It is a fast-paced existentialist play, with snappy dialogues, quick exchanges and quick interchanges – a Theatre of the Absurd tragicomedy in three Acts.

I do not wish to insult my kind audience by saying too much about the play. It is my intention to allow each to draw his or her own conclusions, all of which, I am certain, shall be insightful and correct. It is an open-ended play from which you can derive and deduce what you see fit. It may appear to be a little rough around the edges at times. While the lack of refinement may at times be down to this being amongst my first attempts at writing, it is also intended by way of emphasising on the dysfunctional and the bizarre. The characters and their oddities add to this, and, I hope, make them memorable. It may seem difficult to relate to them at times, but they, like all of us, are ordinary human beings going through the motions and living regular lives; this makes it easy for us to be able to identify with them.

The Deliverance of Sanctuary is riddled with religious undertones, but it is by no means a religious play. It is supposed to lead people towards a religious interpretation, but such an interpretation itself would not be entirely correct because the play is nothing other than absurd. Other similarly erroneous interpretations would be "journey of life", "journey of self-actualisation", "vindication of organised religion", "mockery and criticism of organised religion", "salvation (seeking, or story of)" etc. What it truly represents in spite of the ever-present double entendres, however, is absurdity, since all things being equal, the simplest solution is the best (in this case, absurdity). The misinterpretations that the play deliberately misleads the audience into thinking as being correct collectively epitomise the absurdity of life and every man's crusade to give a greater value, meaning and purpose to a life devoid of all three. Nothing ever truly happens, despite the best efforts of all concerned. Sanctuary is the unattainable hope of every man for something new and different that will grant life a deep-rooted worth.

I had a lot of fun writing this play. I sincerely hope that you are able to enjoy it just as much, and earnestly believe that you shall find it interesting and intriguing. As with all art and literature, it is very personal and dear to its architect. It is my personal plea to my gracious audience that they open themselves up to it and take it in. You will augment my life and my education by doing so, and for that you have my undying gratitude.

Yours,

Ikhtisad Ahmed

CAST

Man in white suit
Doctor
Woman in evening gown
Adam, a boy in rags
Eve, a girl in a frock
A Jester
A Knight
A Court Advisor

Act 1

ACT 1 Scene 1

A Doctor in a white coat sitting at his desk, busy working on some papers. The desk has a phone sitting on it. There is no other furniture in the room. A crisp and neat Man dressed in a white suit, white shirt, white socks, white tie and white shoes, knocks on the door on right of stage. The Doctor asks the Man to come in without looking up from his papers. The Man duly walks in, closes the door behind him and stands in front of the desk, and moves very little. [The Man is expressionless at all times]

Doctor:	(*without looking up*) Hello, why don't you take a seat?
Man:	Good morning doctor, I prefer to stand, thank you. Can you help me?
Doctor:	Good morning. Well, I am quite sure I can. (*looks up at the Man*) But surely, you are too healthy to be ill?
Man:	I know. But you see, illness is all in the mind.
Doctor:	That is very true. You are a very intelligent person sir. (*gets up to examine the Man*)
Man:	You mistake me. I mean to say that I am mad.
Doctor:	(*sits back down, startled*) Sorry, I don't think I got you.
Man:	You did doctor, your startled expression reveals the fact that you heard me clearly, but you do not want to take what I said into account. Since you insist, I shall repeat myself. I am insane.
Doctor:	No, of course not. I mean, of course. I mean…well, if there is a problem then I will most definitely do my part to help.
Man:	Excellent doctor. Then could you please refer me to the mental institute on top of the hill?
Doctor:	(*becoming serious and suspicious*) That is not a madhouse sir, it is a place of refuge for people who have special thinking patterns and thoughts. It isn't called Sanctuary lightly.
Man:	Of course it is not doctor. It is salvation, a God in a Godless world. Is that not what is said about it?
Doctor:	I don't quite follow. (*returning to his papers*) Anyway, you are perfectly healthy.
Man:	I know that doctor, and I am reassured by you not having checked me. However, you are overlooking the fact that I have no physical illness. The imperfection of my human form lies in my head. I am abnormal.
Doctor:	(*dismissing the Man*) Sir, you are a perfectly healthy person.
Man:	But I know that.

Doctor:		(*looks up at the Man quizzically and frowns*) Then I don't quite understand why you have come in to see me.
Man:		I am not sane, and hence I would like to retreat to the mental institute on top of the hill.
Doctor:		But that place…
Man:		I know doctor, I know. And because it is the God, I would like to bathe in its glory. Are you a believer doctor?
Doctor:		Sorry sir, I don't see what that has to do with anything.
Man:		You are not doctor, are you? Of course not. If you were, you would not wear such a monstrous cross around your neck.
Doctor:		I…(*looking towards his chest, then looking up at the Man again*)… What?
Man:		You see doctor, people are blind, and surgeries to implant donated eyes do not make them see either. But then again, the ones who are truly blind are the ones who see. You know that doctor, do you not? They see it feelingly, they are the ones who truly see. The surgery blinds them because it gives them sight, and by seeing, they are truly blind. Why would they want to become impure?
Doctor:		Sir…
Man:		…For the same reasons that you are most likely to step on a new pair of shoes, because if you did not step on the shoes, there would be no necessity for soap to clean them. You truly know the value of something when you lose it, hence to comprehend purity, one needs to become impure. But one does not wish to cleanse oneself once one is impure; one simply wishes to clean oneself in order to recede into the world. Man is not wise enough to comprehend purity, and you cannot value something that you do not understand. Thus you strive towards impurity while ascertaining a clean appearance to convince yourself of your normality and to justify your wrongs.
Doctor:		(*slightly irritated*) Sir, I don't understand what you are trying to say, and I'm not sure that I want to either. I would, however, like to clarify about me being impure, or a believer, or…

[During the man's diatribe, the doctor reacts at first by trying to interrupt him, then by getting annoyed, and finally by becoming mesmerised by the man's words. The man seems oblivious of the doctor's existence and actions throughout]

Man:		Of course! You have to forgive me for trailing off on a tangent doctor. You are an intelligent man doctor, you cannot be a believer. A believer in a Godless world is a fool trying to convince himself that it is not his fault. How can it be his fault when there is a Being beyond him and his world? Everything in the universe is a product of cause, and has a resulting effect. Therefore, whatever happens is caused by someone, and that someone is to blame. God

	cannot defend himself, so let us blame Him. By blaming Him, we acknowledge His existence and become a believer. Yet we are of the conviction that this is a Godless world, otherwise there would not be so much evil and wrong in it. Thus we believe in something that is not there, and there is a collision of two figments of our imagination because they run into contradiction at the moment of their expression.
Doctor:	(*standing up and interrupting*) I've heard of intriguing illnesses that toy with people. But it never occurred to me that they could toy with the doctor too. Sir, if I may…
Man:	You do not seem like such a man doctor, there is an inside to you. You have substance doctor, I do believe that you are not a believer. That cross is merely a demand of society that you have given in to, but nobody is perfect, and so you are entitled to that shortcoming. However, doctor, I do hope that you have considered the school of thought that you have accepted by embracing this demand. You have accepted faith, but have you considered that being a curer of men contradicts with the essence of God?
Doctor:	(*sitting back down, stunned*) What?
Man:	Surely you must have. You cure because there is a God who sends diseases. Are you not the God then doctor, the cleanser? I am God too, I cleanse the world of the entity that is mortals. God is about faith, and you have faith in yourself the same way I have faith in myself. So there is no doubt that you and I are both Gods. If we are both Gods, and there are more like us out there, either the world is full of Gods, or it is a Godless world where we all pose as God or make up a God to introduce another dimension, a false Being that is beyond our comprehension, yet Whom we understand completely. A Being who makes us, defines us and helps us.
Doctor:	(*getting annoyed and standing up to show the Man to the door*) Yes, well sir, I don't see your point, and I'm sure I don't want to either. Sorry if that displeases you, but I really don't have time for this. There are patients that need attending to, and illnesses that need curing. I'm not so sure that either exists in this room right now.
Man:	(*does not move*) Does He help us though doctor? Why would you be waging war against Him with your magical cures if He were helping us with the ailments in the first place? Much like the blind men, is it not doctor? Impurity only to clean, but never to cleanse. If that is so, then you are a false God, as false as the God that your cross represents. You wear the cross to become perfect. I see you are an apt pupil of Aristotle doctor, working towards being that perfect or complete being instead of saying that something is good because it agrees with desire or values. You must know of Plato then too, doctor. He laid out the purpose of humans as defining what the possibilities of human achievements are instead

	of defining what good is. Of course we cannot define good when there is no good, when the God that we believe in, Who talks of good, is not good Himself. Is the world then not Godless?
Doctor:	Aristotle? Plato? (*returns to his desk and sits down*) I…Yes, that is all very good sir. Now, if you will sit down and fill out…(*gets paper out of the bottom drawer of his desk*)…this form, I will arrange for you to meet with the doctors at Sanctuary.
Man:	You think I am mad doctor? Mad is am ambiguous word, I mean insane. You think I am insane because of what I said? You are mistaken my good man, I am indeed insane, but we all are. We do not know what normal is, nor do we know what sanity is. Hence we are all abnormal, all insane. You are right though, I am mentally handicapped, and in spite of you having got the reason for coming to the conclusion wrong, I will not argue since I am overjoyed at you seeing the light that I have been shining at your face. (*bends over to fill the form out*) Thank you very much for your assistance doctor, I envy you. That would be a deadly sin, but this is a Godless world, and you are not a believer, so I will not go through the pains of falsely excusing myself. You envy me too since I am going to Sanctuary, but you have not sinned either, so there is no need for you to be courteous and apologise.
Doctor:	You are mad!
Man:	No doctor, I am not, insane perhaps, but even then not for the reasons you think.
Doctor:	Yes, I mean insane. You are. If you are not insane, then God is dead…I mean then I am not a doctor.
Man:	That is not so unbelievable doctor. Might I suggest, "If you are not insane then I do not exist." The essence of life is existence, and one dare not challenge that. (*hands the completed form to the Doctor*)
Doctor:	I will dispatch you to the mental institute on top of the hill immediately. (*scrambles to make a phone call*)
Man:	Do not rush yourself doctor, you need not hurry because of my dying need to go to the mental institute on top of the hill, let me not hasten you.
Doctor:	No, not at all, it is my pleasure, you don't have to die to go there. (*puts the phone down to look for something*) If I could only find the number…
Man:	426 668 623
Doctor:	I…Thank you.
Man:	You are most welcome doctor.
Doctor:	(*reaching for the phone after having scribbled the number*) They will be pleased with you sir, you are dressed for the occasion, and your intellect would leave them in awe for sure.
Man:	You do not truly feel that way doctor, but I thank you for your kind words. However, you do not have to console me; the convict

	who turns himself in to hang from the aged oak does not wish to be consoled for he is a substantial man whose consolation lies in his substance.
Doctor:	(*putting phone down after having dialled half the number*) You are not insane.
Man:	Am I not doctor? You have concluded rightly that I am, it is advisable and appreciable that you stand by your notable conclusion.
Doctor:	(*squinting suspiciously at the Man, as if searching for something on his face*) No, you are not mad, you are playing me to go to the mental institute on top of the hill.
Man:	I would not dream of doing such a thing doctor. If I offended you by talking only about the male gender, do accept my heartfelt apologies. I am not a chauvinist and would never discriminate. It is just that talking of one gender avoids confusion while having a conversation. Masculine means feminine in statutes, it is much the same while indulging in a conversation.
Doctor:	(*picking up the phone again*) Right, I will sort this out for you in a minute sir.
Man:	I knew you would not turn away from the light doctor. I shall wait outside while you make all the arrangements. My regards to your missus – yes, the ring did not escape me. Good day doctor, and once again, thank you very much.

Exit Man to through the door on right of stage, closing the door behind him.

Doctor:	Could I please speak to Dr. Velnias?…Yes, I will hold on, thank you…Dr. Velnias? How are you sir?…I have a patient for you… You will have to excuse me, I don't have his name (*searching for the form*)…yes, he has filled in a form…excellent, I will send him on his way right away. What was that? Yes sir, I will post the form to you…Yes sir, thank you.

Doctor puts the phone down, takes the form in his right hand, then gets up and walks out of his room, leaving the door open. End of Scene.

ACT 1 Scene 2

The Man is sitting on a block of wood big enough to allow two people to sit side-by-side outside the doctor's office. He is still, unmoving. A Woman in an evening gown enters. She moves towards the Man, stops five paces away and stares at him. He does not look up. They are frozen in this state for a while. Then he looks up at her, his face blank, and returns her blank stare. [The Man is expressionless at all times]

Woman: Are you a doctor?
Man: No madam.
Woman: Then are you a lawyer? You are dressed like one.
Man: No madam.
Woman: Then what are you?
Man: I am mad.
Woman: Are you mad at me?
Man: No madam, I am insane.
Woman: Oh, that is alright then. What are you doing here?
Man: I am waiting, that is what I do, sometimes.
Woman: Are you waiting for the doctor?
Man: No, I have seen him.
Woman: Oh good, he must have treated you then.
Man: He has been very nice to me. I want to go to the mental institute on top of the hill, and he is being most helpful in my cause.
Woman: What is this place?
Man: Have you not heard of the mental institute on top of the hill? That is most unsettling.
Woman: Why so?
Man: It is said to be the most incredible place on earth, a place of refuge and salvation. It is an enlightened paradise.
Woman: (*getting interested*) Really?
Man: Yes, it is the place where the whole of humanity is accepted after self-realisation. A most fascinating place, perched on the summit of the highest point of the town.
Woman: (*enthusiastically*) Can women go there too? Are we all treated equally?
Man: Of course women are most welcome after they have seen themselves for what they are. And we are most definitely treated equally, everyone is insane there.
Woman: Would I have to be crazy to go there?

Man:		You already are. All that is required of you to do is to look in a mirror and see yourself through the window to your soul, shed of all the false materialism of this town.
Woman:		(*looking concerned*) Where can I find a mirror?
Man:		That is a very good question.
Woman:		Will I not be vain if I look in a mirror? Stare into an empty creation of mortals that stares back at you with a depiction of your own form for self-satisfaction?
Man:		You are a god amongst men madam, you belong in paradise.
Woman:		Then I shall wait with you. You know where it is, and if I belong there, then that is the direction in which I shall head.
Man:		That is a most joyous pronouncement.

Enter Doctor from left of stage with the form in his hands. He walks to the woman who is standing. The man does not rise, but instead blends into the background.

Doctor:		Madam, you must be here to see me.
Woman:		No, I am waiting.
Doctor:		Then you need not wait any longer since I am here to serve you.
Woman:		But I am waiting.
Doctor:		Yes, and you don't have to any more.
Woman:		But doctor, I am waiting with this gentleman to be led by him.
Doctor:		(*looks at the Man and understands everything*) Ah, you wish to go to Sanctuary?
Man:		Yes, she is an epitome of the divine beings in this superficial world, and nothing short of the mental institute on top of the hill will suffice her.
Doctor:		(*turning away from the Man, but acknowledging his presence at all times*) That is all very well, but are you mad?
Woman:		I have no reason to be angry at you doctor, you seem to be a wonderful person.
Doctor:		No, I was asking whether you are abnormal or not.
Woman:		I am told that we all are.
Doctor:		(*sighs in resignation*) Very well, if this man here thinks you are worthy of Sanctuary then I'll forward you to its gates as well.
Woman:		You are too kind doctor.

Exit Doctor to left of stage.

Woman:		I should have worn my Sunday best if I had known I was en route to the asylum.
Man:		You were wise not to. One needs to rid oneself of the material inhibitions of the town before entering sacred ground.

ACT 1 SCENE 2

Woman:	You are right! How thoughtless of me not to have realised that! (*she moves towards the block of wood*)
Man:	Yes madam, but it is only fitting for you to have mistaken. That shows that you are mortal in spite of being divine, and are hence worthy of being welcomed to Sanctuary. (*he gets up as he speaks*)
Woman:	You are an enlightened man, and I am very fortunate to have met you. (*she sits on the block of wood*)
Man:	On the contrary, it is my pleasure to be graced by your presence and intellect, I hope to be influenced by it.
Woman:	You surely will, and I hope to be shown the way to the mental institute at the top of the hill by you.
Man:	A most beneficial partnership, very mutual and compatible.
Woman:	I couldn't agree with you more.
Man:	Shall we get married then?
Woman:	That would be ideal, except (*thinking for a minute*) I don't know a minister.
Man:	You are a believer?
Woman:	No, what is that?
Man:	How wise you are.
Woman:	(*looking thoughtful*) But how do we get married then?
Man:	Do you have a ring?
Woman:	I have one on my third toe.
Man:	That will do just fine.
Woman:	Do we make an oath?
Man:	That would not be right since there is no external entity looking upon us to witness and judge our promises. Do you have parents?
Woman:	Not that I know of. But you are right, an oath would be blasphemous.

Enter Doctor from left of stage without the form.

Doctor:	You are both…
Man:	Doctor, would you be so kind as to do the honours?
Doctor:	I'd be delighted to! What should I do?
Man:	We are getting married. Will you oversee it?
Doctor:	(*looking serious and excited*) Most definitely! What book should I get?
Man:	What is your most used and trusted book?
Doctor:	(*without hesitation*) My medicine book of course!
Man:	Then bring that please.

Exit Doctor to left of stage.

Woman:	He is a very nice person. (*rising*) We should make ourselves ready before he comes.
Man:	You are right. What is there to do?
Woman:	(*taking her left shoe off and pulling the ring off*) Now you get your ring, and stand on my right. Then we wait for the kind doctor to return.
Man:	(*takes off his right shoe only to find that he cannot see any rings. After a moment's pause, he takes his sock off and sees a ring on his second toe. He takes it off then goes and stands on the woman's right*)

Enter Doctor from left of stage with a fat book.

Doctor:	(*holding the book up with both hands*) Here is the book.
Man:	Thank you doctor, now we shall get married.
Doctor:	Which page should I read?
Man:	The page about the mental institute on top of the hill.
Doctor:	An excellent choice. (*gets busy looking through the book to find the page*)
Man:	Do you have water doctor?
Doctor:	I can go get some if you want. What for though?
Man:	We have to drink to the occasion.
Doctor:	Of course! I will go get some glasses and a bottle of water right away.
Man:	After we are wed doctor, after we are wed.
Doctor:	That would be better I suppose. (*buries himself in his book again to find the page*) Yes, I have got it, I had it marked all along!
Man:	Excellent, now we can get started madam.
Woman:	You must sit doctor, we would not want you to be uncomfortable.
Doctor:	I am fine madam. Should I begin?
Woman:	Please do.
Doctor:	"The mental institute on top of the hill is almost eternal. It has stood erect and untouched on top of the hill since time immemorial. It is a holy place, a sacred place, and the best of men and women walk there. It is bright because the elevation makes it immune to the fog that the entire town is engulfed by all the time. It is Sanctuary, and proven souls are welcomed graciously after proving to be mad." Do you both agree to join it?
Woman:	I do. (*puts ring on the man's fifth toe on his right foot*)
Man:	I do. (*puts ring on the woman's fourth toe on her right foot*)
Doctor:	Very good! Now you are man and wife.
Man:	Also woman and husband.
Doctor:	Very true...(*closes the book carefully*) You may kiss.
Woman:	Yes, that has to happen since we need to have a baby.

Man:	That is indeed imperative in knowledgeable lives lived in Sanctuary and away from the hells of the town.

They kiss.

Doctor:	Very good, very good! I will now go fetch a bottle of water and some glasses.
Man:	We shall not keep you then.
Woman:	No, we can't.

Exit Doctor, holding the book with both hands, to left of stage.

Woman:	If we have a girl, we will name her Child.
Man:	I was thinking about the same name in the event of it being a boy. We are settled on the name then, it applies to both genders.
Woman:	It is a beautiful name.
Man:	It reflects the innocence of infants. Alas how that is jaded when adulteration is forced upon them. But the baby will not have to endure that since it will be brought up in Sanctuary. It will be wise and free of all the evil in the world, a good human being.
Woman:	(*with pride and joy*) Oh yes, how wonderful that will be! I can't wait for it to be born. But should we not have a boy and a girl?
Man:	Yes, you are right, we need to spread the goodness.
Woman:	Should we not kiss again then? That will allow us to have twins, and then one will be a boy and the other a girl.
Man:	You do not cease to intrigue me with your brilliant mind madam. We should do as you suggest.

They kiss again.

Woman:	Oh! Now we have to think of names for our infants because we will have two now – one boy and one girl.
Man:	You are right.
Woman:	I read a book when I was young where there were many names.
Man:	Did you like the book?
Woman:	I would like it if I could. It said a lot, but not much of it seemed to be true. Either that, or I couldn't understand any of it. Or perhaps I understood it, and therein lay the problem? I can't remember. But it had some nice names in it though.
Man:	A fascinating piece of literature it seems. Do you remember what it said?

Woman:	Well, it did have a fairy tale about how our world came into being. Do you think the town really came into being in that manner?
Man:	All things come into being in a similar fashion. If that is true, then indeed this town came into being in that manner. What else did it say?
Woman:	Nothing else of any interest to me…But it had some very nice names.
Man:	Let us hear some then.
Woman:	My favourite were Adam and Eve.
Man:	That suits our needs to perfection. One a name for a boy, the other one for a girl.
Woman:	How true! This is delightful! It all seems to have been meant.
Man:	You are indeed an amazing person madam.
Woman:	So we are set on the names?
Man:	Yes, they were mentioned in the book for a purpose, and you were meant to read it to fulfil that purpose. It all falls into place.

Enter Doctor, without the bottle of water or the glasses, from left of stage.

Doctor:	I…
Man:	Why doctor, how pleasant it is to see you again. Did you not have something to tell us before we asked you to wed us?
Doctor:	Yes, I did. I came to give you the good news of both of yours admission to Sanctuary. I would advise you to make your way to it as soon as you can. Turn right when you leave the hospital, and you will come across a fork in the road. Take the left fork and keep on the road. That will take you straight to the mental institute on top of the hill.
Man:	You are mistaken doctor, the road will eventually find its way to the asylum after winding and turning according to its predestined shape. And we must follow the path and be led by its preordained nature.
Doctor:	You are right! I'll leave you to it then.
Man:	Thank you very much doctor, you are too kind. (*turning to the woman*) Come madam, we must embark on our pilgrimage.

They just stand there. Exit Doctor to left of stage. The man and the woman remain standing in the centre of the stage. Then they finally move, and exit to right of the stage.

Enter Doctor, with the bottle of water and the glasses, from left of stage.

Doctor: (*distressed*) I didn't give them the water! Good heavens, I didn't give them the water! Goodness me, they didn't drink the water! (*pauses to look around*) But where did they go? Where are all the people? (*looking out at the audience searchingly*). Is there no-one there? No substantial human being? Have they all made their way to Sanctuary? Impossible, that place is for the roses, not the thorns. (*becoming calmer*) Ah yes, I see now (*squints at the audience*) the thorns. But of course! We are all thorns. (*becoming alarmed*) I am left with all of my kind, no substantial people! (*looking up to the heavens*) Yes, it all makes perfect sense, the roses go to the mental institute on top of the hill. How can it be that the man and the woman are roses when they have engaged in copulation? But of course, there is no sin in this Godless world. (*laughing maniacally*) Of course there is no sin for we are all sinners, but that is alright because there is no God to judge or guide us. And how could I forget that they tied the knot before they sinned. So they nullified the sin, but that doesn't matter because there is no sin. It all makes sense now. How could I have been so thoughtless? Or was it that I needed that man to tell me all? It is done, and now I must undo it. (*walks towards the exit to the left of the stage, and tears off the cross around his neck. Stops and looks over his shoulder at the audience*) Can it be that I see the light after all? Or is it that I am mad? I will call Sanctuary and ask for permission to be allowed into it. I come, I come.

Exit Doctor, with the bottle of water and the glasses, to left of stage.

Enter Doctor, with a piece of paper in his hands, from left of stage.

Doctor: Sixth hour of the sixth day, the Devil condemns…All is lost, the number has been erased…(*pauses*) What number? What is this paper? What have I been saying? What am I doing? Did something pass? (*looking at the audience again*) Who is next to see me? Is there anyone there who needs to be purified? Cured? Treated? Anything? (*looks searchingly at the audience*) The horror! There is no purity! All have been tainted I see. I will not tarry any further then. Patients, march! I will now be virtuous because patience is a virtue, and I will give my undivided attention to all that wish to see me. I will deliver purity! If I am lucky, I will even come across a patient who can tell me what just happened, because I don't recall anything.

Exit Doctor to left of stage. Lights fade. End of Scene.

ACT 1 Scene 3

It is darker than previously because it is later in the day. Enter the Man and the Woman from left of stage. Barren land – one bush on the right of the stage and a tree on the left. They keep walking towards the centre of the stage. Suddenly, the Woman stops. [The Man is expressionless at all times]

Woman:	Wait, we must wait.
Man:	Yes, that is what I do, sometimes.
Woman:	But we must wait.
Man:	We shall wait then.

They sit down to wait.

Woman:	But nothing is happening.
Man:	Of course, we are waiting.
Woman:	Wait, I can sense something.
Man:	But I am waiting, that is what I do, sometimes.
Woman:	That is good, but I can sense something happening, so hold on.
Man:	Hold on to what?
Woman:	Wait.
Man:	But I am waiting, that is what I do, sometimes.
Woman:	Yes, good.
Man:	Excellent.
Woman:	Brilliant.
Man:	Exquisite.

Enter a ragged looking boy, staggering, from right of stage. Both the Man and the Woman stare at him, the Woman with concentration.

Woman:	There, something has happened.
Man:	What has happened?
Woman:	A boy has come into this world.
Man:	Ah yes, something has happened.

The boy feels his way to the Man and the Woman, who are still sitting on the ground.

Boy:		(*to the Man, feeling his face*) What are you doing?
Woman:		(*standing up*) Who are you?
Man:		(*looking up at the boy*) I am waiting, that is what I do, sometimes.
Boy:		(*to the Woman, feeling her face*) I am a boy. (*to the Man*) Why are you waiting?
Woman:		(*to the boy*) Where did you come from?
Man:		(*to the boy*) She said that something will happen, so we must wait…I am waiting, that is what I do, sometimes.
Boy:		(*to the Woman*) I was dropped by the stork. It was supposed to deliver me to my parents. (*to the Man*) It is good to wait.
Woman:		(*to the boy*) Oh! You must be Adam.
Man:		(*to the boy*) Thank you boy, you are intelligent.
Boy:		(*to the Woman*) Who is Adam? (*to the Man*) You are welcome sir, and thank you too.
Woman:		(*to the boy*) Adam is our son, and you are Adam.
Man:		(*to the boy*) You are more than welcome boy. Do you think it will rain today?
Boy:		(*to the Woman*) Yes, you're right, I am Adam, who is your son. (*looking at the ground, deep in thought, the to the Man*) I don't know sir, but I don't think it will. Do you think it will rain?
Woman:		(*to the boy*) Yes, you are Adam, who is our son. That means that I am your mother, and my husband is your father.
Man:		(*to the boy*) You are wise indeed. I do not think it will rain either. It rained the day before yesterday, and the day before that. It also rained yesterday, and there are dark clouds forming today. But I do not think it will rain because it rained yesterday, and the two days before yesterday. Since you think not as well, I am certain that it will not rain. But wait, do you just think that it will not rain, or do you will it?
Boy:		(*to the Woman*) Yes! You are my mother! The stork did deliver me to the right place! And your husband is my father. (*to the Man*) I don't think it will rain, and since I don't think it, I will it.
Woman:		(*to the boy*) Yes…Where is your sister, our daughter?
Man:		(*to the boy*) Excellent. I will it too. Then we have nothing to fear, it will not rain for sure. But how will we get water then?
Boy:		(*to the Woman*) My sister is coming. I was told that she was in the mental institute on top of the hill when I departed, but the stork carrying her might take longer to come because of its age. She was to be born first though, so the stork must have lost its way. (*to the Man*) You want water sir? I want it too. If it doesn't rain, then we will have to think of some way of getting water.
Woman:		(*to the boy*) She will come, that's all that matters. (*looks around. Moves around searchingly. Looks into the audience thoughtfully*) It

	all looks barren and dead. It should rain to wash away the filth and give way to birth and life.
Man:	(*to the boy*) Yes, we will have to think of something. However, it can wait. Tell me boy, who are you?
Boy:	(*to the Woman*) You're right! But we just willed it not to rain today. Do you also will it not to rain today? (*to the Man*) I am Adam.
Woman:	(*to the boy*) Yes, it is dreadful to walk in the rain, and the mud also slows you down. I will it not to rain today, but I will it to rain soon, rain is needed to bring life out there (*motioning towards the audience*), in the town. Your births must be welcomed in that manner too.
Man:	(*to the boy*) So you are Adam. That would mean you are my son, and I am your father and my wife is your mother. Where is Eve?
Boy:	(*to the Woman*) Then it'll definitely not rain today. I also will it to rain soon, before I get thirsty. (*to the Man*) Yes, you are my father! Who is Eve?
Woman:	(*to the boy*) Yes, and the water will bring life.
Man:	(*to the boy*) Eve is your sister, and you are Eve's brother. I am the father of both of you, and my wife is your mother.
Boy:	(*to the Woman*) Yes, we do need the rain to come then, we need the water. What are you doing? (*to the Man*) Oh! She is coming from the mental institute on top of the hill. She was supposed to be born first, but the stork must've gotten lost.
Woman:	(*sitting down again*) I am sitting.
Man:	(*to the boy*) Yes, I remember, infants come from the mental institute on top of the hill. She comes from there the same way you do. But you did not know that because you are blind and cannot see.
Boy:	(*to the Woman*) Are you waiting too? (*to the Man*) What is "see"?
Woman:	(*to the boy*) Yes, I am waiting as well as sitting.
Man:	(*to the boy, paying no attention to what he has just said*) But you do see, you see it feelingly. You are truly from the mental institute on top of the hill if you can see feelingly. But you are physically blind, because your eyes do not serve the function they are meant to, and hence you cannot feel it seeingly. But that is alright, you are chaste.
Boy:	(*to the Woman*) Are you waiting because you are sitting, or sitting because you are waiting? (*to the Man*) What are "eyes"?
Woman:	(*to the boy*) I am waiting and sitting. I was walking with my husband, but my instincts hurt, so I knew that you were going to come. So we decided to wait, and I sat to welcome you to the world, to the town. Thus I am waiting and sitting.
Man:	(*to the boy*) Eyes aid you to see in a different way, and the perspective they have allows you to feel it seeingly…(*raises his fisted right hand and sticks out the index, middle and ring fingers*) How many fingers?

Boy:	(*to the Woman*) Can I wait too? (*to the Man. Searches for the man's hand with his hands. His left hand finds it, and he feels the shape carefully*) You have three fingers that are opened.
Woman:	(*to the boy*) Yes, you can. What a good and polite boy you are! Of course you can accompany your mother in her wait.
Man:	(*to the boy*) Excellent. You have come a long way boy, you should sit and rest yourself.
Boy:	(*to the Woman*) Thank you. (*to the Man*) Thank you. (*turns around facing the audience and sits down*)

Silence. The boy assumes the posture of the Buddha meditating. No-one moves.

Woman:	(*turns to face the Man*) I have seen Adam, he is here.
Man:	(*turns to face the Woman*) Your and my son Adam? Yes, I have seen him too.
Woman:	He is a good boy.
Man:	Yes, a fine boy.
Woman:	He said that Eve is coming as well.
Man:	Yes, she comes from the mental institute on top of the hill, same as he.
Woman:	(*getting excited*) Has he come from Sanctuary?
Man:	He has indeed, all infants come from there.
Woman:	Oh! Do tell what he has to say about it!
Man:	What would he have to say about it?
Woman:	(*excited and impatient*) What is it like? How glorious is it? What is it like to live there?
Man:	He is an untainted soul. And he knows nothing of the sort.
Woman:	(*looking confused*) Why not?
Man:	He is physically blind, and hence feels Sanctuary but does not see it. Thus, he is, of course, a pure soul, uncontaminated by all the filth of the town, untouched by all the unsubstantial dispositions.
Woman:	(*disappointed*) Oh! That is a bother! Don't you want to know what Sanctuary is like? Are you not curious?
Man:	I know all that is required to be known by mortals about the mental institute on top of the hill. Should I know more, I will be one of the divine beings in it. What is curious?
Woman:	That is a feeling, the emotion of being eager to learn, as I read in a book.
Man:	(*completely unenthusiastic*) I see…
Woman:	Should we wait for her?
Man:	Wait for whom?
Woman:	Eve, should we wait for her?
Man:	Who is this "her" you speak of?
Woman:	Eve. Should we wait for Eve?

Man:	Are you feeling her arrival approaching?
Woman:	(*pausing to think*) No, I don't.
Man:	Then we do not have to wait for her till you can feel it.
Woman:	Very true! But shouldn't this be our temporary home? Of course we are moving, so it is only our home for now, nothing permanent. But we found Adam, and so this should be our home for now.
Man:	You are absolutely right. We are moving, and so this cannot be our home indefinitely. This is the home that we are leaving for our new home in the mental institute on top of the hill. But this is our temporary home.
Woman:	Excellent! (*looking up*) Do you know whether it will rain today?
Man:	No, Adam and I willed it not to rain, so it will not rain today.
Woman:	Did you? I willed it not to rain today with Adam too! But only today, because it needs to rain soon.
Man:	You are right. What a wonderfully wise lady you are.
Woman:	Thank you sir, but your existence eclipses mine. (*pauses*) Night draws near.
Man:	Yes, it fell upon us when we left the doctor and embarked on our quest.
Woman:	Has it been that long?
Man:	Is it long?
Woman:	I don't know.

Silence.

Man:	What are you going to do?
Woman:	I'll sleep a while because night has fallen. (*lies down*) I am also exhausted from the birth.
Man:	Yes, that needs to be done since night has indeed fallen.
Woman:	What are you doing?
Man:	I am waiting, that is what I do, sometimes.

Silence as the Woman falls asleep. Adam closes his eyes, still remaining in his posture. The Man waits. Lights fade. End of Scene.

ACT 1 Scene 4

Lights begin to come back on dimly because dawn has broken. Woman asleep, Adam motionless in his Buddha-like posture. Man sitting casually and waiting. Looks up as if something has struck him all of a sudden. Makes as if to get up, then doesn't. Ponders something. Reaches the decision to get up. Moves across to the right of the stage, but in no hurry. Looks around; glares at the audience and moves behind the bush. [The man is expressionless at all times]

Man: (*coming out of the bush, buttoning up his jacket and brushing it to make sure that everything is in order. Comes to the front of the stage and stands, thinking, with the Woman and Adam over his right shoulder, and the bush over his left*) One can get all sorts of answers from nature. It calls, and when it does one must answer its call. (*looks over his right shoulder to the Woman and Adam, then slowly looks over his left shoulder at the bush. Turns back and resumes his thought*) Yes, the call of nature has to be answered. Some are fortunate not to have been called from their slumber, but when they awaken they surely will be, and the call will be one that will necessitate a quick answer to prevent any accidents. (*pauses to think*) I wonder if the swallow will fly today…or perhaps winter is in the air and the ducks will make their pilgrimage. Alas, if only man had such a purposeful journey as the ducks, but man was never meant to be a pilgrim. I, the man, have let the anchor down on the serene waters of the night. But morning comes and the anchor must be withdrawn to continue on the voyage. (*looks up at the sky, perhaps looking for the sun; keeps gazing up*) Yes, the moment of re-embarkation draws near. (*raises a finger to point at the sky and slowly brings it down to point at the Woman and Adam as he speaks*) Behold, the message is conveyed and the world awakens.

The Woman and Adam wake up. Adam remains in his posture and yawns, while the Woman sits up.

Woman: Are you still waiting?
Man: No, I was answering nature's call.
Woman: I have awoken, so I must too. (*gets up and rushes towards the bush. Man keeps looking up in thought. She returns shortly and joins him in his gaze*)

Man:	What are you doing?
Woman:	What are you doing?
Man:	It would appear the same as you, but what are you doing?
Woman:	Undoubtedly the same as you, but I don't know why.
Man:	(*looking at the Woman*) I was trying to find the North Star to aid us in our journey. It appears to be playing a childish game of hide and seek with me.
Woman:	(*looking at the Man*) I was looking to find the clouds to see if it will rain.
Man:	Rain? That would make this day rather delightful, would it not? It will be the perfect foreground to the backdrop of the canopy that is the sunlit sky. A chasm of many depths.
Woman:	Were we not headed East?
Man:	Yes, it would be perfect indeed.
Woman:	Then why do you search for the North Star?
Man:	East you say? Yes, that is where our destination lies, the mystic East. Pray how know you?
Woman:	The rain would ruin the road to walk on, but it would make a pretty sight.
Man:	You must know because you are gifted. Are you from the East yourself?
Woman:	The East? Oh yes…I mean no.
Man:	Many a word means many a thing, but this is indeed a strange use of the word 'yes' that I see. A positive to mean a negative – how modern.
Woman:	I have been there. I went with that book to tell the stories of the book. But getting to know the East made me forsake the stories for a greater cause. The place was dark, yet light emitted from it. I was lost in all the wealth of the place and was plunged into a great abyss. I came out a new person, although I wasn't able to understand all that was told to me…no, not told, shown…no, not shown, said…no, not that, but…well, anyway, I didn't understand it. So I came out perplexed and returned to the West, further into town. Order was restored, but life never was.
Man:	The great East, how I will to find you. I stumbled upon it on one of my errands for the mayor, but I skimmed it instead of going through or into it. Your experience has indeed been enlightening. It makes me sure of the fact that I want to go there, and glad of the fact that I am going there. But how know you that we are headed East?
Woman:	Because you can't find the North Star.
Man:	Such logic. You are indeed fascinating. Yes, that is correct, we are headed East, to the divine place…to our destination.
Woman:	Weren't we three last night?

Man:		Three? Nay, we were one, but there were three of us. The boy sleeps there. (*motioning towards Adam. The Woman follows his pointing*)
Adam:		I am awake father, but I am missing a tooth.
Man:		Your tooth is your sister now, she will come soon.
Adam:		That is…
Woman:		(*interrupting*) Did you sleep well son?
Adam:		(*to the Woman*) Yes, I think I have, and so I have. I dreamt of a silly thing.
Man:		Was it a funny thing you dreamt of?
Adam:		(*to the Man*) Perhaps. I dreamt that you had come to town in my form, to give yourself to the town.
Man:		Humorous story, devoid of any meaning, sense or relevance. It is worth writing though, it is sure to appear in the book of our lives' quest.
Woman:		What a funny story! Children are full of such wonderful ideas! Had I had that dream I would have laughed in it…except then I would be really laughing too, which would have caused me to wake up.
Adam:		(*to the Woman*) I would have laughed, but I was father, and father was me. But the world laughed. A third person in me was saying it was a wasted laugh, but I knew it was wrong because I wanted to laugh, which meant father wanted to laugh, and father is never wrong. In the end it came to light that the laughter was right…all those who didn't laugh were hanged from a hill above a hole full of fire. I couldn't make out whether I was hanging too because I hadn't laughed, but just as I was beginning to wonder whether father and I being the same had saved me I was awoken to answer the call of nature.
Man:		Yes, your biology tells the tale. (*moves towards Adam*) To your feet, (*helping him get up*) I will lead you to answer the call. (*takes him to the bush and waits as he goes behind it*)
Woman:		I can feel her coming.
Man:		Yes, I thought the time was ripe. But you shall linger a while, and she will come at your time for we have created her.
Woman:		How true that is! Adam must be present alongside you and me as she arrives.
Man:		Yes, he must finish his business before she can enter the world.

Adam comes out of the bush and grasps thin air, trying to find the Man. The Man extends his hand and they move towards the Woman.

Man:		You must lie down as she enters.
Woman:		Yes, but I am lingering. It is not time till we decide it is.

Adam:	What is happening? I feel something. The space seems to grow smaller because there seems to be more of us now.
Man:	You will share soon, but not till it is time; and it will be time when we decide that it is time.
Adam:	I will wait then. I will be patient about losing my loneliness.
Man:	Loneliness is not when you are left alone by the world, but when the world is left alone by you. It is make-believe. The term you look for is solitude, and in solitude you find solace. But fear not, your solitude will remain. It will become the seclusion of two entities which will extend its hand to all others and let them all be overcome by it. Wait till we reach the mental institute on top of the hill before you spread the light though, that is the beginning and the end, and the sole existence, of light. That is where you belong.
Woman:	Can it be time now?
Man:	(*looks up*) Yes, it can be.

The Woman lies down in anticipation of the arrival of Eve.

Adam:	Nothing is happening. I can't see anything.
Man:	You say you cannot see? But that is not possible, you are the one of sight.
Adam:	I shall try harder…wait, something comes…

Enter Eve from right of stage.

Woman:	(*breathing heavily*) She came by harder than Adam, Eve is too easy a name!
Man:	Or too suitable. Come here my child. Do not be afraid, this is a strange place you have chanced upon, but order will be restored – we shall return to your place, we are in the midst of a journey there as we speak.
Adam:	Speak? But she hasn't said a word, has she?
Woman:	Sorry, it is the shock that caused me to lose speech. But I am fine now. I have been restored to my former self.
Adam:	That is a relief mother. But she doesn't speak.
Man:	(*moves towards Eve, who is still shy. He looks up as he walks towards her and pauses part way there*) The clouds part and the sun shines down. Perfection of nature, something sinister awaits.
Adam:	Speak child! Speak, or forever hold your peace!
Woman:	You have the sight Adam, Eve will have the speech. I heard your father tell of people from the mental asylum on top of the hill.

	He said they are perfect beings. I see the truth in his statements now.
Man:	(*still gazing up*) A statement that is true you say? You speak of a miracle happening. You are either delusional from Eve's arrival or it is the East in you that speaks.
Woman:	Miracles? I remember the word…vaguely. Is it not one from the book?
Adam:	Sorry mother, but I didn't read it, so I don't know. (*lowers head in shame*) You must be very disappointed in me.
Woman:	(*laughs*) That's not possible son. You have a long way to go, you will come across the book and many more in due time.
Man:	(*unfaltering in his gaze*) Yes, there is indeed a long way to go. The road is lengthy and the lessons countless. A long way to go – you will learn.
Woman:	Oh my, we forgot all about Eve…
Man:	No, we did no such thing. We have welcomed her, it would be rude not to give her time to get acquainted with her forgettable surroundings.
Adam:	May I go and have fun with her?
Man:	(*still looking up*) Fun? What is that?
Woman:	Yes you may. But be gentle, she is fragile. (*Adam goes towards Eve. She is apprehensive at first, then welcomes him with a smile. They start to play*)
Man:	(*still not looking down*) Ah, fun – a thing of the mystic East I see. But I doubt she is fragile, she has strong teeth. That would have to mean she is of hard stock.
Woman:	Are you still checking the weather? You could try to get that from the news.
Man:	(*continuing to stare at the sky*) Yes, I did read the news once. There was a story about the mayor being religious and wanting to wage a holy war against someone else, who sounded all too imprudent for me to have given him any heed. The nonsense of it made me quit for fear of finding myself to be a regurgitating child.
Woman:	Oh my! That was not pleasant at all. (*curiously*) What more was there to the news?
Man:	(*content at finding what he was looking for and looking back down*) No, not the weather madam, that takes its own course as its life dictates it to, for all non-living things are dictated by life, unlike all things living which dictate life, or ought to at least. It is when the latter allows life to dictate that they take the form of the former. But to return to your question, I was not checking the weather; I was checking to find truth in my intuition, but alas that is as much of a mystery as it always has been. Are you healed? Shall we continue our journey?
Woman:	(*getting up*) Yes, I am gathering strength. We can move on.

Man:	(*moving towards the Woman and giving her a hand to get up*) Shall they be called?
Woman:	Yes, and I will help Eve wash up before we travel.
Man:	Delightful idea. I shall sit down and anticipate your return. (*sits down*)
Woman:	(*to Adam and Eve*) Adam, Eve, we must be going now. There is a long way to go your father says, and we must move before the day grows old on us. (*to Man*) Will you be waiting then?
Man:	No, that is what I do sometimes, but it will be unwise to do so when one is sitting in anticipation of the return of two.

Adam and Eve come and join the Man and the Woman.

Woman:	What a splendid thought! (*turning to Adam and Eve*) Come Eve, we must clean up before we travel. You sit in anticipation of our return with your father Adam.
Adam:	(*sitting down*) I will do that mother.

The Woman and Eve move to behind the bush to clean up. The Man and Adam sit in anticipation of their return.

Silence

The Woman and Eve return.

Adam:	Footfall…they must be returning.
Man:	(*getting up*) Yes, they have joined us once more. We must continue our journey now. (*helps Adam up*)
Woman:	Yes, we are both ready.
Man:	Shall we?

Exit Man, Woman, Adam and Eve to right of stage, the Man holding Adam and the Woman holding Eve. End of Scene.

ACT 1 Scene 5

It is brighter than the previous Scene because it is later in the day. A Jester wearing a motley sitting on a dead tree-trunk in the centre of the stage sharpening a knife on the trunk.

Enter Man from left of stage.

Looks at Jester emptily. Goes towards him and stands on his right. Stares at him. Jester doesn't pay any attention to him. [The Man is expressionless at all times]

Jester:	Did you lose something?
Man:	No.
Jester:	Then do you have obsessions in the bent?
Man:	What is that?
Jester:	Never had a sense of humour, did you?
Man:	What a delightfully polite person you are.
Jester:	Sarcasm is the lowest form of wit you twit!
Man:	It is still wit though, is it not? But sarcastic I am not sir.
Jester:	(*getting irritated*) Shut up!
Man:	That defeats the point and purpose of a conversation though, does it not?
Jester:	Why in God's name are you still staring at me?
Man:	God is a name that is but a blur, a clouded frontier that grants a shade to the eye that makes a man look through grey glasses onto a battlefield and a woman through pink ones onto a bed of roses.
Jester:	(*annoyed*) Stop staring at me!
Man:	But you confuse a look for a stare my good man.
Jester:	Aren't you even remotely scared of a man holding a knife getting angry at you?
Man:	That would be rather foolish. A man may wet himself and a woman may cry for help, but I find them to be rather superfluous acts. A child is more intelligent in such situations – a child would merely stare inquisitively.
Jester:	(*paranoid*) There! You just said the word! Stare! Stare! Quit staring at me!
Man:	But I am not staring sir.
Jester:	You just said you are!

Man:		No, I said a child would stare at a man holding a knife inquisitively, and I said that would be the right thing to do rather than what a man or a woman may do in the same situation.
Jester:		That doesn't matter! What matters is that you are staring at me, and you must stop that!
Man:		What a long knife you have sir.
Jester:		(*getting distracted*) Yes, it is nice. You like it?
Man:		It would be rude not to. What is its use?
Jester:		(*getting irritated again*) To cut things up with you idiot, what is a knife used for?
Man:		It is also used to cut through things, and cut into things.
Jester:		(*annoyed*) They are all the same! You stupid fellow, the important word is "cut", not "through", "into" or "up".
Man:		How right you are! I was being silly in sacrificing the significant facts for the minor details.
Jester:		Yes, now get going, go find yourself some corner to cry about your mistake.
Man:		Where shall I find a corner in this open ended world? Corners are found in closed, angular objects.
Jester:		(*paranoid*) For God's sake shut up! Or...(*looking around*)... or...(*looking at his hands and seeing the knife*)...or I'll give you a demonstration with the knife. The tree liked it too before I let him have it.
Man:		The tree was a man?
Jester:		Good Lord! Are you a man? Men sure don't talk as much as you do!
Man:		Whatever it was is resting in peace now. It was nice of you to be kind and generous in your actions to it.
Jester:		Yes, it was, and I'll be the same to you if you don't shut up!
Man:		You will be nice to me? That would be going out of your way kind sir, for neither do you know me, nor have I done anything for you. Let me thank you profoundly.
Jester:		(*getting distracted*) Why you're very welcome. What's the occasion?
Man:		I was going to ask the same of you sir, but the aberrations of your weapon warned me off.
Jester:		Yes, she is pretty, isn't she?
Man:		It would be rude to disagree with the truth. What does it do?
Jester:		(*getting annoyed*) L-o-r-d! What is wrong with you? You are stupid and you make no efforts to make amends for it!
Man:		You are very wise sir, you must be the envy of the world.
Jester:		Yes, I better be! Now shut up and get going you silly little man. Go pat an old lady on the head and ask her to make you some tea.
Man:		Yes, they are having tea. I came to scout ahead. Would you like to come join us?

Jester:	(*slightly worried and scared*) Good Lord! Are you schizophrenic too? Is there anything about you that is right or good?
Man:	Right and good are very different sir, but on both counts, not much I'm afraid, but enough to allow me to enter the mental asylum at the top of the hill.
Jester:	You are beginning to make me very mad.
Man:	That is excellent! Then you too may come with us to the mental asylum on top of the hill.
Jester:	(*getting up*) You are a disgrace to humanity! You deserve to be put to the sword you scum!
Man:	Yes, pity you have no sword.
Jester:	You dare mock my weapon?
Man:	No sir, but a knife is hardly a sword. Calling a knife a sword would be like calling a dead tree alive.
Jester:	(*getting ready to strike*) Shut up! Shut up! Shut up! Shut up and I might let you live you filthy little adulterer.
Man:	Hardly adultery whence the act of marriage precedes indulging in procreating. Copulation is marginal sir Jester.
Jester:	(*completely taken aback as if struck a hard blow*) How do you know what I am?
Man:	That is not what you are sir, it is who you are, and yes, I do know who you are.
Jester:	(*scared*) How do you know what I am?
Man:	I know who you are for a man's essence lies in who he is, and it is of utmost importance to know the essence of a man.
Jester:	(*scared and desperate*) How in God's name know do you know why I am?
Man:	How clever of you! Adding the words "in God's name" vainly in an attempt to disguise the same question as being completely different.
Jester:	(*desperate and paranoid*) Answer you demon from hell! Answer the question you devil incarnate!
Man:	Of course, there being a God automatically gives birth to a devil. You must pity whoever was pregnant with that, being the believer that you are.
Jester:	(*takes a few steps back, astounded and scared*) How do you know I am a believer? How?
Man:	Because you do not wear a cross.
Jester:	(*triumphantly*) Hah! You are wrong you human excretion! My knife is my cross!
Man:	That is very unique of you sir, but if I may draw your attention to a minor detail that is of major significance and cannot be overlooked in the greater scheme of things, you are not wearing your knife and you are hence not wearing your cross.

Jester:	(*enraged*) How dare you question the intentions behind my cross! The tree could have been a vampire which would require the use of my cross! My cross! To bear! And to bare as I will!
Man:	Vampire you say? Delightful thought, especially coming from a believer.
Jester:	I…not another word, lest I banish you to the circles of hell!
Man:	But sir, that will hardly get you to the mental asylum on top of the hill.
Jester:	I don't want to go there! Sending you to hell would be doing a service to the Lord, and that would book my place in heaven.
Man:	Killing gets you to heaven sir? Extraordinary.
Jester:	Not simply killing you brothel-frequenter, killing for a purpose, and in the name of God!
Man:	But sir, would the mental asylum on top of the hill not be the place you want to go to, for you say you are mad.
Jester:	I am not mad! (*emphatically*) I am not mad!
Man:	But you were once, were you not?
Jester:	(*takes a few more steps back, as if struck another blow*) How did you know I was once there?
Man:	There? Where?
Jester:	(*irritated and scared*) There you fool, there! The mental asylum… there!
Man:	(*giving a blank stare at the audience*) You were once there?
Jester:	There? You mean at the mental asylum?
Man:	At the mental asylum on the top of the hill you ask? Why do you ask? Were you there?
Jester:	(*annoyed*) Stop repeating yourself for God's sake! Stop!
Man:	But I ask you separately sir.
Jester:	You are insane!
Man:	That is why I go to the mental asylum on top of the hill and not there, for the former is where all life and meaning exist while the latter is where death thrives amidst the horror of so-called life.
Jester:	(*impressed*) You mock very well fool.
Man:	Hardly sir, that would be very well done by a true fool.
Jester:	You are discriminating by attributing particular qualities to specific groups.
Man:	Forgive me sir, I am not wise for I have not been to the mental asylum on top of the hill. Your knowledge comes from that holy place, but mine from the opposite, and there they typecast all.
Jester:	(*calming down*) I forgive you because you have depth. Yes, I have been there.
Man:	Where?
Jester:	(*irritated*) God! To the mental asylum on top of hell I tell you!
Man:	Ah yes, and would you like to go there with us?

ACT 1 Scene 5

Jester:		No! They did away with me for my desire to be stereotyped! All men are equal there.
Man:		And women?
Jester:		(*confused*) Who ever said Marx was a woman?
Man:		That he was not, but he referred to mankind when he said man while you mean it as a chauvinist.
Jester:		(*proudly*) Fools are chauvinists, but I am not.
Man:		There is a flaw in how you typecast sir, or there is a flaw in the reflection of the type that I see.
Jester:		(*falls to his knees, as if struck another blow*) You correct me? You dare correct me? A mechanism of the devil dares correct me?
Man:		Emphasis by repeating, but trusting in the three.
Jester:		(*paranoid and scared*) Trying to avoid the subject won't save your soul! I demand an explanation!
Man:		I shall provide you with one then. "Thrice I ask you, and thrice you say no…Thrice I seek answer, thrice you seem to know…Thrice I get up, only for there thrice to be a blow…Thrice I see light, and thrice the light does flow…"
Jester:		(*sarcastically*) Bravo! You're a poet and you don't know it, stupid waste of human matter! (*gets up*)
Man:		Is sarcasm not the lowest form of wit?
Jester:		(*annoyed*) Shut up! For God's sake shut up and give me an explanation!
Man:		You ask me for two things which are contrary and not complementary. Pray which do you want me to do?
Jester:		Shut up!
Man:		But that defeats the point and purpose of a conversation.
Jester:		Explain!
Man:		Ah – that I would gladly do within my earthly limits, for I am not yet a soul of the mental asylum on top of the hill. What would you like explained sir Jester?
Jester:		Explain…(*pauses to think*)…I have forgotten. (*panic-stricken*) Good Lord I have forgotten! I have forgotten! I am such a fool!
Man:		Calm yourself sir. A fool you are, but there is a remedy for the forgetting.
Jester:		(*paranoid*) I have forgotten! Forgotten! (*staring at the audience*) I have returned to the basic entity of the place that is there! I am one of them now! (*scared*) God help me, I am one of them now! I am a non-entity! Forgotten! (*screams and runs off the stage, exiting into the audience*)
Man:		He has gone back to the place of futility, forsaking the place of fertility that we journey towards. Shame he did not have his tea or stay for dinner. Shame. (*stands on top of the dead tree-trunk and looks out at the audience, silent and in deep thought. Remains there*

for a while, then gets down and moves towards the exit to right of stage. Glances at the audience one last time) Shame.

Exit Man to left of stage. Lights fade. End of Scene.

ACT 1 Scene 6

A Knight wearing a medieval armour and an Advisor wearing a ruff and a black robe sitting, facing one another. The Knight is sitting on a rock, while the Advisor sits on a raised piece of the ground. They each seem oblivious of the other's presence.

Advisor:	(*looking at the audience in thought*) Sir Knight, we are one short in our party.
Knight:	(*looking distracted*) He will come sir Advisor, he will come.
Advisor:	(*looking around at the audience*) Come he might, but my patience is on the wane. We have waited for a while now, and yet he appears not.
Knight:	(*still looking distracted*) He will come, sir, he will come.
Advisor:	How long has he been away for? I cannot even recall that. Perhaps my memory is on the wane too. That would be a shame, there is so much I have no records of that I very much would like to remember.
Knight:	(*glancing towards the two entrances of the stage*) Are we looking in the wrong place?
Advisor:	(*turning his attention to the Knight*) No, for we are not looking. We are waiting, and there is no place in respect to that. It is an act. The act is right, the place of this sacred act is irrelevant.
Knight:	(*turns towards the Advisor*) Forgive me sir, you are right.
Advisor:	No, that remains to be seen. I hope that I am, but we all do I suppose. We all live in hope and hold on to it for dear life. (*turning towards the audience*) However, I would like to know whether I am right or not, which is why I am still waiting for him. He will know. But I do hope that I am right.
Knight:	(*awe-stricken*) Profound. That is why you are the advisor, and I am but a humble knight.
Advisor:	(*continues to look at the audience*) Each has his own gifts. What you lack in brains, you make up for in brawn. Appreciate it, doing otherwise would be disrespectful to him.
Knight:	Perish the thought! I would not even think of keeping him away.
Advisor:	(*turns back towards the Knight*) Are you though? Did you ask it of him?
Knight:	No, I did not pray for such a distasteful thing.
Advisor:	No, that you did not. But did you ask for it to happen?
Knight:	Does it matter?
Advisor:	Did you though?

Knight:	You must forgive me sir! I did not mean to do so! I was under the impression that it was of no relevance!
Advisor:	Did you ask of such a thing?
Knight:	My will does not control him, he is beyond that. You, sir, you, though, can perhaps control him with your superior thinking.
Advisor:	No, I cannot do such a thing. He cannot be kept away by sheer will, or by thought nor strength.
Knight:	Then he will come, he must.
Advisor:	Yes, and we must wait. (*turns back towards the audience*)
Knight:	How right you are! You must write!
Advisor:	I shall, I shall. If I am right, I shall write. The right has to be preserved and passed on.
Knight:	Passed on? How?
Advisor:	There are creatures out there who will welcome it, and embrace it.
Knight:	(*mockingly*) Yes, and I will turn into a sheep that will be sacrificed in my stead.
Advisor:	(*in a light-hearted manner*) You mock me good sir, but you speak the truth, as do I. It will all happen, all of it, and more.
Knight:	That I can neither disagree with nor mock.
Advisor:	It is not in your place to mock, that is for another to do.
Knight:	Yes, the truth will happen, he will come.

Enter the Jester, from the audience, frantic, frightened and out of breath.

Knight:	He is here! He comes! He is here!
Advisor:	(*still looking at the audience*) Yes, but though our party is complete, we are still missing one. Without him we are incomplete.
Knight:	Sir Jester! Where have you been?
Jester:	(*running up the Advisor and the Knight, panicking*) I have forgotten! Forgotten! I have returned to the basic entity of the place that is there! I am one of them now! God help me, I am one of them now! I am a non-entity! Forgotten!
Knight:	(*looking at the Advisor, confused*) What is he talking about?
Advisor:	(*turning his attention away from the audience and towards Knight and the Jester*) That was bound to happen.
Knight:	(*still confused*) What? What?
Jester:	(*pausing, running from one end of the stage to another, then running to the Advisor and the Knight and pausing again. Looks towards the ground in thought, then looks up at them*) Ah, the two of you. I let the tree have it!
Advisor:	That was bound to happen.
Knight:	(*still confused, but not raising his voice*) What? What?

Jester:	That old hag will not be playing courtesan to any more mindless, odious idiots that travel on that road.
Advisor:	That was bound to happen.
Knight:	(*still confused, but not raising his voice*) What? What?
Jester:	Yes, and I'm proud to have put an end to that. May the ones who miss it, or insist on laying hands on it despite it being fallen, be stricken by a plague.
Advisor:	You speak of the best laid plans.
Knight:	(*finally cracking the puzzle*) Ah, that.
Jester:	Laid, and best laid! No-one can interfere with his plan.
Knight:	Do you not mean to say "this"?
Advisor:	No, he means "his".
Jester:	(*sitting down*) Yes, his plans, for which we shall be greatly rewarded when he comes. (*pausing, and looking horrified all of a sudden*) Or has he come already?
Advisor:	No, rest easy good sir, we are still waiting.
Jester:	(*visibly relieved*) That is a tremendous relief!
Knight:	Yes, we still await his coming. (*looking excited*) He will surely lead us down the barren, thorn laden path to our fiery destination. We have done enough to deserve that ultimate reward for which we all have lived. It will only be the right sort of justice.
Advisor:	(*turning towards the Knight, slightly disturbed*) You speak of things which should not be spoken of. We will each be weighed and measured, and we will each be judged accordingly. It is also not in your place to know about the path and the destination. Be aware kind sir, for you may be disappointed with the conclusion that you have prognosticated once you see the reality as that may be very different indeed.
Knight:	(*to the Advisor, still excited. The Jester, by now, is also excited, and he too focuses his attentions on the Advisor*) Forgive me for my thoughtless words about the path and the destination, I spoke of suppositions. But surely, we will not be found wanting?
Advisor:	That is not for us to decide. We can only do what we must. We must not concern ourselves with anything else. We live our lives regardless of what will happen later. That irrelevance will take care of itself.
Knight:	(*letting the Advisor's words sink in, and understanding them*) You speak the truth. We shall live then, and wait.
Advisor:	Yes.
Jester:	Yes. But what of the mental institute on top of the hill?
Advisor:	(*looking towards the Jester, thoroughly confused*) What? The what? What?
Jester:	The…
Knight:	(*following in the Advisor's footsteps and feeling the same*) What?
Jester:	Yes, that's right. That.

Advisor:	(*seemingly understanding*) Ah, that.
Jester:	Yes, that.
Knight:	Yes, that.
Advisor:	So we are all agreed?
Knight:	(*to the Advisor, enthusiastically*) Of course we are! There are no other paths, and there are no other destinations!
Jester:	(*to the Advisor*) I agree! He has already spoken of the unspeakable path and the unspeakable destination which we don't live for, but which he will hopefully lead us to when he comes.
Advisor:	(*to the Jester*) The path and the destination? You know? Why, then, did you not correct sir Knight?
Jester:	(*confused*) I know? What do I know?
Knight:	(*to the Advisor, looking hopeful*) You agree with me then sir?
Advisor:	(*to the Knight*) No sir, I cannot agree with you until the truth is shown to me.
Knight:	You are right, of course you are. Silly of me to assume!
Jester:	Yes, quite.
Advisor:	(*to the Jester*) So you do not know then, sir, do you?
Jester:	(*to the Advisor, inquisitively*) Know what?
Knight:	(*to the Jester*) About the path and the destination.
Jester:	(*to the Advisor*) Which path? And what destination?
Advisor:	(*looking away from the Knight and the Jester, and at the audience*) That is the question kind sir, that is the question.
Knight:	(*looking from the Jester to the Advisor*) Didn't he ask two?
Jester:	I did, but sir Advisor caught the essence.
Advisor:	(*continuing to look at the audience*) I could catch the essence if words had essence.
Knight:	(*to the Jester, eagerly*) So do you know about the path and the destination?
Jester:	(*to the Advisor*) Which path? And what destination?
Advisor:	(*continuing to look at the audience*) Those are the pertinent questions that need to be answered. I am relieved not to stand corrected.
Knight:	Indeed!
Jester:	So we are settled then?
Advisor:	(*looking back at the Knight and the Jester*) Yes, very good. We all live in hope, and we wait.
Knight:	Yes!
Jester:	Hope?
Advisor:	Yes, him.
Knight:	(*to the Advisor, hesitantly*) Who is "him"?
Jester:	(*to the Advisor, seeking clarification*) What does he have anything to do with anything?
Advisor:	(*to the Jester*) You said hope, did you not?
Knight:	(*to the Advisor, unsure*) Did I?
Jester:	I asked, yes.

Advisor:	(*triumphantly*) Exactly! Him!
Knight:	(*to the Jester, confused*) You asked? About him? About whom?
Jester:	(*realisation dawning on him*) Oh, him? I have met him.
Advisor:	(*taken aback*) You have what?
Knight:	(*urgently*) Gentlemen, I must know before my bladder runs lose!
Jester:	(*confused*) Did I not? Meet him that is? Did I not?
Advisor:	You could not have! We have been waiting for him here!
Knight:	(*urgently, growing frustrated*) Yes, you are right. So have you two answered my questions?
Jester:	Waiting here you say? (*pausing, deep in thought*) Of course you have! And I set off to let the tree have it!
Advisor:	Yes, you did, and you returned after having accomplished your mission. So you could not have met him. Since he has not shown himself while you were away, neither you nor we have missed anything. We can rest easy now.
Knight:	(*looking distressed, then pausing, looking confused*) Do you mean hope?
Jester:	That is a relief! But can we really rest? Would that be wise?
Knight:	(*becoming calm all of a sudden*) He said it, and he is wise. Therefore, what he said must be wise.
Jester:	(*turning towards the Knight for the first time*) Your brain is sharper than your brawn today sir Knight, I applaud you for making it all make sense to me.
Knight:	(*bowing*) Thank you sir Jester, but not stronger than yours.
Jester:	Do you mean my brain or my brawn?
Knight:	Brawn of course. You let the tree have it, while I have wasted my strength.
Jester:	Yes, so it would seem. You have not wasted your brain, however, and I applaud you.
Knight:	(*bowing and remaining prostrated*) I thank you.
Advisor:	(*standing up*) I stand corrected.
Jester:	(*turning towards the Advisor*) Yes, you do.
Knight:	(*standing upright and turning towards the Advisor*) Yes? Do you?
Advisor:	Yes. We cannot rest. We must wait.
Jester:	Ah, of course! It is all so clear to me now!
Knight:	You are wise, sir, so you must be right.
Jester:	Yes, you must!
Advisor:	Quite. (*turning towards the Knight*) How is your bladder sir?
Knight:	(*suddenly becoming distressed again*) It needs relieving!
Jester:	Very good, very good. So we are settled then?
Advisor:	Yes, we are. We shall wait.
Knight:	No, we must.
Jester:	Indeed!
Advisor:	Yes, we must wait.

They continue to stand and wait. Lights fade. End of Act.

Act 2

ACT 2 Scene 1

It is getting dark. The Man is sitting on the fallen tree, looking towards the audience without any expressions. He gets up and slowly walks towards the edge of the stage. [The Man is expressionless at all times]

Man: Night approaches, and it still has not rained. No sign of it at all. Alas, if this keeps up then we will be going to the top of the hill to fetch a pail of water. We are four in our company, not two, so a pail may not suffice. Unless…(*thinking*)…unless the lady and I go. That should solve the riddle. It looks like going to the top of the hill is certain to be purposeful. That is sure to be to everyone's satisfaction. I shall now wait for the others to arrive to tell them of this delightful development. (*goes back to the fallen tree, feels it to make sure it is there, and then sits down on it again*)

Enter the Doctor from left of stage, dressed in a kesa, wearing the Papal Tiara on his head, two crosses (one Protestant and one Catholic) and the Star of David around his neck, and a set of Muslim prayer beads around his right hand. He also has a Hindu swastika painted on his forehead. The Man ignores the new arrival, and gazes at the audience.

Doctor: (*looks around searchingly, walks around the stage ignoring the Man completely, finally sees the Man and walks towards him with his back to the audience*) What are you doing?
Man: (*looking up at the Doctor*) I am fine, thank you. I am waiting.
Doctor: What good will come of that?
Man: What evil will come of it?
Doctor: I don't think any will. Nothing can come of nothing.
Man: Valid observation. But something can come of waiting.
Doctor: You agree, then you disagree. Waiting is nothing, therefore nothing can come of it. Unless you are waiting for someone, or something?
Man: That I am indeed.
Doctor: You are right then, something will come of your waiting.
Man: But nothing will come of yours?
Doctor: I am not waiting. I am travelling.
Man: That is a good hobby. You have changed much from the last time I saw you doctor.
Doctor: (*looking concerned*) Are you talking to me?

Man:	(*looking around to make sure there is no-one else around*) It would appear so doctor. Had I not come to you the last time we met, this pleasant occasion would mark you coming again.
Doctor:	(*relaxing*) You are mistaken my friend, I am no doctor.
Man:	Not of the body perhaps. You seemed to be when I saw you last, but I may have been wrong. A doctor of the mind then, for certain. Your diagnosis suggests it.
Doctor:	I see that my reputation precedes me. I can assure you that I am no doctor, certainly not of the mind, which is why I travel to meet Dr. Velnias. What are you doing alone on this weary path friend? I must confess to being quite surprised at meeting anyone at all. You are the last person I have seen since leaving the town.
Man:	Friendship is as good a virtue as any, thank you for bestowing your kindness upon me. I detest being impolite, but I must correct you for I am not alone.
Doctor:	(*looking around to check if anyone else is there, then looking disturbed*) Perhaps you should come with me to see the good doctor too if you think that you aren't alone.
Man:	Will you not sit down? It is more desirable than standing there as you are.
Doctor:	(*looking suspicious, and taking a few steps back*) Yes, yes, you're right, sitting would be more comfortable.
Man:	So you say you are not a doctor? I must be losing my mind. I was certain that you are. Perhaps it is your kindness that deceived me.
Doctor:	I wish I could help you with why you mistook me for a doctor.
Man:	(*interrupting*) Not a doctor, the doctor.
Doctor:	Yes, the doctor. Wait, what did you say?
Man:	The doctor.
Doctor:	(*outraged*) Sacrilege!
Man:	Why so?
Doctor:	You confuse me for the doctor?
Man:	No, I do not.
Doctor:	You said you do!
Man:	No, I did, till you corrected me.
Doctor:	(*relieved*) A timely intervention on my part! I may just have saved you!
Man:	I shall remember that for when I need saving. That is twice that you have been kind to me in a short time.
Doctor:	(*looking suspicious*) How do you know how much time has passed?
Man:	Night approaches, but dawn is further away. I deduced from that that you have been kind to me twice in as many days, which I take to be a short time when talking about the great act of kindness.

Doctor:		Divine act of kindness, yes. I can't fault your logic, it has been a short time. You should consider travelling with me friend.
Man:		To go to meet Dr. Velnias? The name sounds familiar, a mystic name.
Doctor:		You know the doctor?
Man:		I thought I knew him when I mistook you for the doctor, if that is who you mean.
Doctor:		Do you, or do you not, know Dr. Velnias?
Man:		Familiar as the name may sound, I cannot place him. Therefore, I must not know him.
Doctor:		You are from the town then?
Man:		I was from the town, now I am from here.
Doctor:		Curious! What do you mean?
Man:		I went to see the doctor in the clinic in town in order to be referred to the mental asylum on top of the hill…
Doctor:		(*interrupting*) You went to see Dr. Velnias in the town?
Man:		Well, I did not catch his name, but he was a doctor, and he was in the clinic in town.
Doctor:		A doctor you say? That is understandable, could have been any old simpleton. Pardon my interruption, continue, please.
Man:		Yes, I went there, got my referral, and as I was exiting the place I met an extraordinary lady to whom I was married by the doctor.
Doctor:		Mazaltov! (*alert*) Wait, did you say you were wed by the doctor?
Man:		Yes, the good doctor at the clinic in town.
Doctor:		Ah, good doctor you say? At the clinic in town? Must be that same simpleton you were talking about a while ago. Was it the same man?
Man:		Yes.
Doctor:		(*relaxing*) Pardon my interruption again, do continue, please.
Man:		Thank you. So my wife was granted access to the mental asylum on top of the hill…
Doctor:		(*interrupting*) Sanctuary? Do you speak of Sanctuary? Speak up my man!
Man:		Do you mean the mental asylum on top of the hill?
Doctor:		(*exasperated*) Do I mean the mental asylum on top of the hill you ask me? Do I mean that place (*pointing upwards and towards the right*), that place?
Man:		(*following the doctor's gesture*) Yes, it is in that direction.
Doctor:		That is not a place to be spoken of so lightly my friend. Sanctuary it has been since time immemorial, and Sanctuary it will remain.
Man:		That is what I speak of.
Doctor:		You are fortunate to have gained admittance to it, the chosen few. I am travelling to it myself. Since you are alone, and we are friends, perhaps we should travel together? I loathe travelling alone, but the destination is such that company has been sparse.

Man: But I am not alone.

Doctor: (*looking around to check if anyone else is there*) But you are friend, you are.

Man: You are right in that we are all alone. We are born that way to live a life of solitude before dying, alone and decrepit. Of course, there are a fair few who are not fortunate enough to live long enough to be decrepit, or should I say not unfortunate enough to be so, but nothing can be done about the state of being alone. You know all of this? Of course you do. You are wise to be headed to the mental asylum on top of the hill for you are wise, and hence you know.

Doctor: Modesty forbids me to accept your high praise, but thanks, friend.

Man: You are very welcome. I would accompany you on your journey, but I cannot for I must wait.

Doctor: Yes, I remember you saying that you were waiting. Is there anyone you wait for? Or is it some thing that for which you wait?

Man: I am waiting, that is what I do, sometimes.

Doctor: Of course! Of course! Forgive my intrusion on your private matters.

Man: Think nothing of it, you were not to know. You do not have to travel alone, however, should you choose not to.

Doctor: What do you mean?

Man: There was a fool here not so long ago who seemed to know about our destination.

Doctor: A fool knowing about Sanctuary? That's not possible. You jest friend.

Man: I do not, but he does. He does not have a choice because he is a fool.

Doctor: You meant that sort of a fool? Then he would know.

Man: Yes, he does know. He has been there.

Doctor: (*taken aback*) He has been there? Where can I find this divine being?

Man: He left rather urgently in that direction. (*points towards the audience*)

Doctor: Thanks again friend, you have been kind to me (*counting*) twice now. I can never repay you.

Man: You were kind to me as many a time as I to you, so you owe me nothing. It is good that we settled the transaction fairly so as not to burden you with having done so much for me only to get nothing in return. Will you not sit?

Doctor: I can't. I must seek this holy being out. I must depart.

Man: I shall see you in there.

Doctor: You are coming as well?

Man: Our ultimate destination is the same, so I must.

Doctor:		You are right! I'll see you there. (*moves towards the exit on right of the stage, then realises something and stops suddenly*) Wait, I can't leave you here alone, not after you have been such a good friend to me. Perhaps I should sit down and wait with you. (*begins to move back towards the man*)
Man:		That is alright, you should continue. I am not alone.
Doctor:		But you are!
Man:		I am, and so are you.
Doctor:		I am not, not right now. You are here with me, so I can't be alone. But you will be when I leave, so I mustn't. If I do, I'll be left owing you.
Man:		You are alone, just as I am alone. We are all alone. However, that is not what I was speaking of.
Doctor:		What then?
Man:		I am accompanied by others on my travels. It thus follows that you should leave, since your failure to do so will result in me owing you. That will be a most regrettable situation to find ourselves in after having completed such a favourable transaction with such ease earlier.
Doctor:		(*stops*) You speak sense friend. I'll leave now then.
Man:		So you will not sit?
Doctor:		I don't see how I can. I'll see you at our destination. (*turns and moves towards the exit on left of the stage*).
Man:		Where do you go? From whence you came?
Doctor:		No, I go to meet the exalted being you spoke of.
Man:		If that is true, then I regret to inform you that you must alter your course.
Doctor:		(*stopping and turning towards the man*) Why?
Man:		The fool went south, in that direction (*pointing towards the audience*).
Doctor:		(*moving towards the audience*) Then that is where I go.
Man:		Indeed.
Doctor:		What will you do?
Man:		I shall wait, that is what I do, sometimes.
Doctor:		If you think that's best.
Man:		I am told I know so.
Doctor:		Then you must be right. I'll see you later.
Man:		Should you reach the destination, you shall.

Exit Doctor into the audience. Man continues to sit and wait.

Enter Woman from left of stage.

Woman:	So there you are!
Man:	(*feeling himself*) It would appear so.
Woman:	(*moving towards the Man*) What ever are you doing here?
Man:	(*continuing to sit*) Waiting.
Woman:	Why?
Man:	That is what I do, sometimes.
Woman:	Should I wait with you?
Man:	If you think that that is necessary.
Woman:	Is it necessary?
Man:	If you think it is.
Woman:	Should I think it is?
Man:	I am afraid I cannot answer that at the present moment.
Woman:	It might help me to know the answer if you told me why you are waiting.
Man:	That is what I do, sometimes.
Woman:	Were you waiting for me?
Man:	You and you alone?
Woman:	Well, I wasn't alone, so maybe I should rephrase.
Man:	It is for the best.
Woman:	Were you waiting for us?
Man:	Do you mean to ask whether I am waiting for you?
Woman:	No, for us.
Man:	I cannot continue to wait for you since you are already here. As for the boy and the girl, yes, I await their arrival.
Woman:	But they have arrived already!
Man:	(*looking around the stage, searching for Adam and Eve*) I do not see them.
Woman:	They were born yesterday, don't you remember? The stork brought them? I should say storks, because there were two.
Man:	Forgive me madam, I misunderstood you.
Woman:	Women can be difficult to understand.
Man:	They are incomprehensible, but that is not what I meant.
Woman:	I am sorry sir, I must have mistaken what you had said.
Man:	That happens sometimes. I meant to say that I misinterpreted the meaning of "arrive" when you were speaking of the boy and the girl.
Woman:	I see! Wouldn't that mean that I misinterpreted the word to begin with because you spoke it first?
Man:	You are correct. Let us rectify this predicament by choosing our words more carefully. I am no longer waiting for you since you are already here. The boy and the girl, however, are not here. Thus I continue to wait for them, as well as waiting, for that is what I do, sometimes.
Woman:	Were the children meant to be here?

Man: You and I are. Children are never to be left to their own devices, not when they are young. Parents' presence and supervision is not only advised, it is mandatory. So, really, the boy and the girl should be here since we are.
Woman: In that case I shall wait.
Man: Will you not sit?
Woman: (*studying the tree*) Is the tree comfortable?
Man: It is more desirable than standing.
Woman: (*disgusted*) But it has moss and dirt on it!
Man: Yes, it aged considerably before taking its leave.
Woman: That can't be very good for my Sunday best!
Man: I do not recall you wearing your Sunday best.
Woman: (*indignantly*) I'm not. I'm simply saying that it wouldn't be very good for my Sunday best.
Man: You would know better about such things.
Woman: I can't sit on it then!
Man: As you wish.
Woman: (*impatiently*) How long do we have to wait?
Man: Waiting is a permanent state of being. There is no beginning, nor any ending. That is why it is called "waiting". We wait – we continue to do so once we are in that state. There is an incessant need for us to allow its constant flow once we have opened the flood-gates. And then, after a while, we forget when the flow started. Hence no beginning, no ending.
Woman: (*looking concerned and slightly irritated*) That's not much comfort! How am I to know how long I need to stand if I don't know how long we shall wait for?
Man: You do not need to stand at all madam, you choose to do so. Since you will, there is no knowing the duration as it is all dependent on waiting.
Woman: Is there nothing we can do?
Man: While waiting you mean?
Woman: Yes…I mean no…I mean, is there nothing else we can do?
Man: We cannot do anything else while we are waiting since then we would not be waiting any longer. The doing of something else would contradict with doing the one thing, the one thing being waiting. However, if you mean whether there is something else that we can do instead of waiting, and not along with waiting, then your reasoning is flawless.
Woman: So what can we do?
Man: I am waiting, so I do not know of anything else that can be done.
Woman: But we can do something else, isn't that right? You said as much yourself.

Man:	I agree that there is no error with the reasoning that we can do something else instead of waiting. One thing is as good as another since one thing takes as much of our resources to do as another. One might say that one thing is the same as another. You rightly reasoned that we could do something else.
Woman:	So what can we do?
Man:	I am waiting, that is what I do, sometimes.
Woman:	Could we not go look for them?
Man:	You do not know where they are?
Woman:	Of course I do!
Man:	Then we would not need to look for them. We would simply have to go to them.
Woman:	But I thought you said that they would come here?
Man:	They ought to come here, yes. What, though, do children know of logic and reason? Indeed, what do they know of anything? If they knew, they would neither be children, nor be chaste.
Woman:	Should we go to them then?
Man:	Do you not want to wait?
Woman:	I'd rather not. I will to stand, which is a source of discomfort. Things could get worse for me because it might rain.
Man:	Are you certain? I was of the contrary belief.
Woman:	Well, it hasn't rained for…(*thinking*)…since…(*counting*)…since I can remember. It must, soon, which will make it a treacherous journey as I was telling Adam yesterday.
Man:	(*looking up*) I am afraid I still do not see any signs of it, but you may be right nonetheless. It is best not to take any chances with such things.
Woman:	Shall we go to them now?
Man:	Do you not want to wait?
Woman:	No.
Man:	In that case we shall go to them, since that is the only other thing there is to do. (*getting up*) They are safe?
Woman:	I see no reason why not. They were playing when I left them.
Man:	Are they behind or ahead?
Woman:	Ahead. It would be wrong to hinder our journey.
Man:	(*offers her his arm*) Shall we?

Exit Man and Woman to right of stage. End of Scene.

ACT 2 Scene 2

It is darker than it was in the last Scene because it is later in the day. The Knight, the Advisor and the Jester, in the same place as they were before. The Advisor is sitting on the raised piece of ground, while the Knight is sitting on the rock. The Jester is pacing about, pausing, coming towards the front of the stage, looking searchingly into the distance and continuing to pace about the stage. The Advisor seems oblivious of the others' presence, not even looking at them, instead concerning himself with looking at the audience, thoughtful and preoccupied, nodding to himself as if he understands, shifting his weight and checking the exits searchingly every now and then. The Knight follows the Jester with his eyes.

Jester:	(*stopping in the middle of the stage and referring to no-one in particular*) How much longer?
Knight:	Till I need to relieve myself?
Jester:	Didn't you relieve yourself?
Knight:	Not since we set out to meet him.
Jester:	Didn't you say that it needed relieving?
Knight:	What needed relieving?
Jester:	(*getting irritated*) You! Didn't you need relieving?
Knight:	Don't we all? All the time?
Jester:	I am sure that we all do, but not all the time. I don't need relieving, and I haven't needed it for quite some time.
Knight:	Needed what?
Jester:	Relieving!
Knight:	Oh yes, of course.
Jester:	Of course what?
Knight:	Relieving. Isn't that what you said?
Jester:	No, I asked. Enquired, if you will, after your needs.
Knight:	You are cruel to jest so sir!
Jester:	I jest? What a notion!
Knight:	Or a motion.
Jester:	Nay, a creation!
Knight:	From a collision.
Jester:	Leading to fusion.
Knight:	Causing confusion.
Jester:	Only for those who belong to a mission.
Knight:	Our mission?
Jester:	What is it?
Knight:	Our mission you mean?
Jester:	(*getting irritated*) I know what our mission is!

Knight:	Then why did you ask?
Jester:	I wanted to know whether you knew.
Knight:	We are here to do the same, aren't we?
Jester:	If only we were doing something!
Knight:	What are we doing?
Jester:	(*frustrated*) Absolutely nothing. We simply put our feet up and waited.
Knight:	Your feet are still planted firmly on the ground, as are mine. (*looks around*) Although, if there was another rock, I could move it near me and put my feet up since you insist.
Jester:	(*getting even more irritated*) I insist nothing of you!
Knight:	So why did you say "put our feet up"?
Jester:	I said it to use hyperbole to emphasise on the stupidity of this whole situation!
Knight:	Use what?
Jester:	Use…Never you mind. Didn't you need to relieve yourself?
Knight:	So you don't want me to put my feet up?
Jester:	(*on the verge of shouting*) Forget about your feet!
Knight:	I wasn't thinking about them till you brought them up.
Jester:	I didn't bring them up!
Knight:	Of course you didn't, they aren't your feet. You could bring yours up if only you were sitting. Or resting. Or sleeping.
Jester:	Yes, very well, I can't and won't bring anyone's feet up.
Knight:	You can if you want to.
Jester:	(*annoyed and exasperated*) Can we please just let the feet be?
Knight:	Let them fall where they may?
Jester:	Or lie where they fall.
Knight:	I see no reason why not. It is a perfectly acceptable situation.
Jester:	No, it categorically and most definitely is not!
Knight:	The feet?
Jester:	(*angry*) Will you please forget about the bloody feet?
Knight:	(*looking at his feet*) Mine aren't bloody. Are yours? Do you want me to help you with them?
Jester:	No! No-one's feet are bloody. But can we please move away from the topic of feet?
Knight:	It wasn't my choice of topic. I will have you know that it was imposed upon me by you.
Jester:	Yes, alright, yes, it was. (*mocking apology*) I am very sorry for talking about feet, or indeed mentioning feet. Now, the end.
Knight:	Of what?
Jester:	(*nearly shouting*) Of the topic of feet!
Knight:	If you want it that way.
Jester:	Yes, yes, I do, thank you, goodbye.
Knight:	Are you leaving?
Jester:	Only the topic. Don't think I can, even though I want to.

Knight:	Why can't you?
Jester:	Because (*pointing towards the Advisor*) he said we are to wait for him over here.
Knight:	Is he coming here?
Jester:	How the deuce am I supposed to know?
Knight:	Then why are you waiting here?
Jester:	Why are you?
Knight:	Because you are, and because he is.
Jester:	Because who is doing what?
Knight:	Because he is waiting.
Jester:	He won't be coming here if he is waiting, will he? He can't wait and come.
Knight:	Don't we all wait before we come?
Jester:	I would if I were coming, the waiting makes the latter worthwhile.
Knight:	You speak from experience?
Jester:	Of course I do! Do you take me for a fool?
Knight:	Aren't you one?
Jester:	(*annoyed*) I am no dunce! Only an inbred dunce would not speak from experience!
Knight:	So you do speak from experience?
Jester:	Of course I do!
Knight:	In that case, if he has experienced it as you have, wouldn't he wait before coming?
Jester:	(*silent, thinking*) You are right! That must be it!
Knight:	It must?
Jester:	Yes, of course it must! What else can it be? He is waiting before coming! How could I not have seen it before? I am such a fool!
Knight:	No-one blames you for it, it's the role you were assigned. I should be very happy if I were given that role.
Jester:	(*distracted*) Yes, I am such a fool. He waits before he comes, and we wait for him to come. What a good joke!
Knight:	There, see! You are doing a sterling job!
Jester:	(*turning back to the Knight*) I'm sorry, what did you say?
Knight:	I need to relieve myself.
Jester:	Yes, yes, you do, of course you do. I shan't keep you any longer.
Knight:	Why haven't I relieved myself till now?
Jester:	Perhaps because you didn't need relieving?
Knight:	But I have needed relieving since we left to meet him. Since before then. Since I can remember. Since I was born.
Jester:	So why didn't you? Why haven't you?
Knight:	Because…(*thinking*)
Advisor:	(*looking down*) Because you, like sir Jester and I, were waiting, sir Knight.
Knight:	(*remembering*) Indeed! Because I was waiting!

Jester:	(*turning to the Advisor*) He speaks!
Knight:	He speaks to you?
Jester:	Not him! (*pointing to the Advisor*) Him!
Advisor:	(*smiling, but continuing to look down*) I do not recall losing my voice sir Jester.
Jester:	Everyone is a fool these days.
Knight:	I apologise profusely, I never intended it.
Jester:	(*dismissively to the Knight*) Shut up!
Advisor:	(*still looking down*) You will find that he is incapable of doing that, for nor did he lose his voice.
Jester:	(*sarcastically*) Yes, how delightful!
Knight:	Are we still waiting?
Advisor:	(*looking up at the audience*) Yes, we are.
Jester:	But why? Why?
Advisor:	Because he is not here.
Knight:	(*suddenly showing urgency*) What if I need to relieve myself?
Jester:	Do you? Need to relieve yourself?
Knight:	Yes.
Advisor:	Then it is best that you do.
Knight:	Won't he think ill of me?
Jester:	Of course he will!
Knight:	Then…what should I do?
Advisor:	Do what you think is best.
Knight:	(*growing increasingly distressed*) I don't know what is best.
Advisor:	None of us do.
Jester:	He waits before he comes, so if you get your timing right, you can relieve yourself satisfactorily.
Knight:	I…I don't…I…don't…know.
Advisor:	Then you are like all of us.
Jester:	Yes, I'm sure that comes as infinite comfort to him. (*impressed*) How do you sleep at night with all that wisdom?
Advisor:	Since you ask, I struggle, so much so that I have not slept since we embarked on this quest.
Jester:	I'll remember not to ask again then.
Advisor:	You are too kind.
Knight:	(*calmer*) Are we still waiting?
Advisor:	Yes, we are.
Jester:	How do you know that he will come here?
Advisor:	Do you ask me?
Jester:	Yes, I do.
Advisor:	I do not know anything.
Jester:	(*showing his impatience clearly*) Yes, I get that it is not for you, or any of us to know. But do you specifically know anything about his coming?
Advisor:	He is, that I know.

Jester:	Good, good. And is he coming here?
Knight:	He must be if we are waiting.
Advisor:	Very good sir Knight, you are very right!
Jester:	So we continue to wait?
Advisor:	That would seem appropriate.
Knight:	Have you seen him sir?
Jester:	(*frustrated*) How could I possibly have seen him if I have never come across him?
Advisor:	No, I have not.
Jester:	And why on earth would I be waiting for him if I had seen…wait, what did you say?
Knight:	Me?
Jester:	No! Not you!
Advisor:	I have not seen him.
Jester:	Then how do you know what he looks like? (*pointing to the Knight*) For all you know, he could be him!
Advisor:	But I do not know anything.
Jester:	Yes, I understand! What I meant was that he could be him, and you wouldn't know because you haven't seen him.
Knight:	Am I him?
Advisor:	(*looking thoughtfully at the Knight*) I may not know anything, but I do know that he is not him.
Jester:	But how are we to know who he is if we don't know what he looks like? You haven't seen him, so he could be standing in front of you and proclaiming himself to be him, and you wouldn't know whether to believe him or not! Am I the only one who sees the idiocy of this incredulous situation?
Advisor:	I will know.
Jester:	You will know because…?
Knight:	It is a risk he is willing to take.
Advisor:	Yes, it is, and I will.
Jester:	(*exasperated*) Capital!

Enter Doctor from the audience, dressed as he was when he left the Man.

Doctor: I come, I come, my companions, I come.

The Jester, the Knight, and the Advisor turn towards him one at a time, respectively.

Advisor:	So you do.
Jester:	Is that…him?
Knight:	Is it him?
Advisor:	No, it is not, sir Knight, and that is not him, sir Jester.

Jester:	You surely can't know for sure. You said so yourself!
Advisor:	No. I said that I had not seen him, but I said that I will know him when I see him, meaning that I would have no trouble identifying him.
Knight:	Who is he then?
Advisor:	I do not know.
Knight:	But you said that you would have no trouble identifying him, didn't you?
Advisor:	Him, (*pointing to the Doctor*) not him.
Jester:	So it could be him?
Knight:	I don't follow.
Jester:	(*to the Knight, annoyed*) Of course you don't!
Advisor:	But you do sir Knight, we all follow.
Jester:	(*to the Advisor again*) So it could be him?
Advisor:	No, it is not him.
Knight:	I follow.
Advisor:	Yes, you do, we all do.
Jester:	(*hoping against hope*) But it could be, couldn't it? That could be him.
Advisor:	Neither it nor that could be him.
Doctor:	(*coming up to the three, and turning to the Advisor*) Of whom do you speak?
Jester:	Him.
Doctor:	Dr. Velnias?
Knight:	Who?
Advisor:	No.
Doctor:	If that is the case, then you are all mistaken. I am not he.
Advisor:	You are correct, you are not.
Doctor:	We haven't gotten off on the wrong foot then. Excellent!
Knight:	Are your feet into being up too?
Doctor:	Yes, I could do with putting them up. Long have I travelled alone, and long have I longed to rest a while.
Jester:	(*mocking*) You have come to the right place then.
Advisor:	We do not rest.
Doctor:	Then what are you doing?
Knight:	We are waiting.
Advisor:	(*being cautious*) Do not be hasty sir Knight!
Doctor:	Waiting? What good will come of that?
Advisor:	I must look within for counsel before I can answer that. (*closing his eyes and becoming silent*)
Jester:	He has to think it over.
Knight:	In peace, with his feet up.
Jester:	Consult his family.
Knight:	His companions.
Jester:	His friends.

Knight:	His co-inhabitants.
Jester:	His compatriots.
Knight:	His subordinates.
Jester:	His intellect.
Knight:	His books.
Doctor:	(*startled*) His books? Which books?
Knight:	Yes, his books, the ones he has.
Doctor:	You misunderstand me my friend, I didn't ask what books, I asked which books.
Knight:	Are we friends now? That is good news! How kind of you!
Jester:	(*to the Doctor*) How can you expect a fool to know the difference between the two questions?
Doctor:	(*turning towards the Jester*) A fool…the fool!
Jester:	What do you mean?
Doctor:	You are the fool I was told about!
Jester:	What do you mean?
Knight:	He means that you are the fool that he was told about.
Jester:	(*to the Knight, annoyed*) Yes, I know that!
Knight:	Then why did you ask?
Jester:	I asked because…never you mind. (*turning towards the Doctor*) What do you mean by that? Told? Who told you? And what?
Doctor:	I was told by my friend that the fool travelled south.
Jester:	He told you?
Doctor:	Who?
Knight:	I don't think I told you anything.
Jester:	(*turning towards the Knight*) Thank you for clearing that up, you have finally been of some use. (*turning towards the Doctor*) Who is this friend you speak of?
Doctor:	I was travelling alone until I met him.
Jester:	(*growing impatient*) Yes, long have you travelled alone, I understand. Get a move on!
Doctor:	But I have only just reached you!
Jester:	With your tale I mean!
Doctor:	I see. I was travelling alone until I met him, a man, my friend. I asked him to join me on my journey because our destination was the same. He told me that he couldn't because he wasn't travelling alone. However, he said that the fool travelled south, and I should go towards him should I need company because…
Jester:	(*looking suspiciously*) What man?
Doctor:	The man. My friend.
Knight:	(*to the Doctor*) You have more than one friend? Can I be his friend? It would only seem right since the two of you are friends.
Jester:	(*being cautious and suspicious*) What was this man wearing?
Doctor:	He was rather well-dressed.
Jester:	(*getting enraged and pulling his knife out*) I will have your head!

ACT 2 Scene 2

Advisor:	(*eyes still closed*) Calm yourself sir Jester, calm yourself. He means no harm.
Doctor:	(*taking a few steps back*) Listen to the wise man, I don't wish to harm you.
Knight:	(*jumping up and moving towards the Jester*) He is a friend…my friend. (*reaches the Jester before the Jester reaches the Doctor. The two wrestle, the Knight easily overpowering the Jester and taking the knife off him and throwing him to the ground*)
Jester:	(*getting up and dusting himself, then turning towards the Advisor*) How do you know?
Advisor:	(*eyes still closed*) Because he has a well-meaning look about him.
Jester:	That's it? Just because of that?
Advisor:	(*opening his eyes and looking up*) Because of his garb.
Jester:	(*sounding a little convinced*) Is that all he has to gain favour from you?
Advisor:	Because he journeyed to meet you for companionship.
Jester:	Did he now?
Advisor:	Because he has befriended sir Knight. (*walking up to the Knight as he speaks, then taking the knife from the Knight and handing it to the Jester*)
Jester:	(*taking the knife from the Advisor and sheathing it*) Yes, they claim to be friends.
Advisor:	And because he journeys to meet him.
Doctor:	Dr. Velnias? That won't be a chance meeting. It can't be helped, seeing as how my destination is his domain.
Jester:	He means well then?
Advisor:	Yes, he does.
Jester:	And you are sure that he is not him?
Advisor:	Yes, I am.
Knight:	(*to the Doctor*) Are we going to travel with you?
Doctor:	I was hoping to find some company for my journey because…
Advisor:	No, sir Knight, we must wait.
Doctor:	Wait? What good will come of that?
Jester:	We have no choice but to wait, now that you are not him.
Advisor:	Yes, we are waiting for him.
Doctor:	Since you put it that way, I shall wait with you.
Jester:	So we are settled then?
Advisor:	Yes, we are. We shall wait.
Knight:	No, we must.
Jester:	Indeed!
Advisor:	Yes, we must wait.

They continue to wait. Lights fade. End of Scene.

ACT 2 Scene 3

It is darker than it was in the last Scene because night is falling. Adam and Eve are sitting in the middle of the stage, on a desert-like piece of land. Adam has his back to the exit on left of the stage, and Eve has her back to the exit on right of the stage. There are two paths in the backdrop, a fork in the road: the one on the right is descending, and is lush, rich and full of life, while the one on the left is ascending, and is barren, overcast and surrounded by death. Enter the Man and the Woman from left of stage. [The Man is expressionless at all times]

Adam:	(*stops playing and looks up, alert*) I hear footsteps. Be still Eve.
Eve:	(*looks around, confused, trying to understand why Adam has stopped playing. Looks ahead and sees her parents. Smiles*)
Woman:	The Lord of the Manor has returned, the Lord has returned!
Adam:	(*turning around*) Is that you mother?
Woman:	Yes, I have come as well.
Adam:	Who else comes with you? The Lord?
Woman:	Yes, your father, my husband.
Adam:	All three?
Woman:	Yes.
Adam:	But I heard only two sets of footsteps.
Woman:	Your father and my husband are the same person. The other set of footsteps that you heard belongs to me.
Adam:	I see! It's good to know that I am not hearing things wrong. That would severely handicap me.
Woman:	You can always trust your ears my son, they are enhanced not to fail you.
Adam:	It would be cruel if they did.
Man:	It would indeed. Alas, such is the nature of this unforgiving cycle that we so lovingly call life. Your youthful candour is refreshing boy, things must always be as they seem to you.
Woman:	(*to the Man*) But things are never what they seem, are they?
Man:	All other things being equal, things are always as they seem, for that is the simplest, and therefore the best. The boy has learnt it, and learnt it well upon conception. His creation as the being that he now is was completed at the mental asylum on top of the hill. Their alterations have left their mark on him permanently, but that is what has allowed him to see, see it feelingly, and to learn, learn to better understand what is ultimately going to allow his safe return to the same place.

Woman:	To Sanctuary?
Man:	Sanctuary is where you lay madam. It is attained where you are safe, for security identifies and defines it. For now it is here, but I cannot say for certain whether it will remain the same tomorrow as we continue our journey. The boy shall continue it with us, I hope, and so will the girl. They will hence return to the place of their completion, to come full circle, their purpose fulfilled.
Woman:	Until they die.
Man:	We all must, for we are born with one foot in the grave.
Woman:	(*dismayed*) It must be terribly difficult getting by life with just one foot! I should think that very unkind!
Man:	It is, but such is life. Unkind, cruel, unfair. The human condition is tailored to perfect imperfection. That is why most fall prey to pity. Some select few journey to escape the supposed poorer state of pity.
Woman:	And so we soldier on.
Man:	Soldiering on is what they are good at. The world is a battlefield. We take pleasure in killing our own kind. That, of course, allows for the ones akin to our own kind to have more reasons to pity, while the ones responsible for the deaths of our own kind can escape pity momentarily without going through the hassle of journeying.
Woman:	So we soldier on?
Man:	Do you ask me whether we continue our journey?
Woman:	Why?
Man:	Why do you ask me that?
Woman:	"Why" is as good a question as "what", don't you think?
Man:	Is that all you wish to know?
Woman:	I wish to know everything.
Man:	Then I cannot tell you.
Woman:	Why not?
Man:	I do not know.
Woman:	Then how am I to know?
Adam:	Am I to know?
Man:	Perhaps you are not to know. Perhaps you are simply to fulfil yourself by completing your journey. (*thinking*) Yes, perhaps that will give you meaning.
Adam:	That can only be a good thing.
Woman:	(*to Adam*) I think so.
Man:	Can it be a bad thing?
Woman:	(*to the Man*) I can't see what, or how.
Man:	Then it must be a good thing.
Adam:	I am happy to hear that!
Woman:	(*to Adam*) You should celebrate with your sister.

Adam: Thank you mother, I'll return to our game. (*begins to play with Eve again*)

Woman: That is a very good idea!

Man: Yes, he is not ill-conceived.

Woman: (*to the Man*) How could he be? We did as recommended, prescribed even! We followed every word, so he couldn't have been ill-conceived.

Man: Every word of what madam? What did we follow?

Woman: The book.

Man: Which one?

Woman: The one I had read long ago, almost in a past life. Except it couldn't have been in a past life, because then I would be immaterial now. Except the first life can be immaterial if one isn't careful, and doesn't live with substance. However, substance is given in the human form, while it isn't within. (*feels herself*) So that couldn't have been my past life, and neither is this, because I can't have a past life, only a present one, and, more importantly, a future one.

Man: Your future, like mine, is death. You will cease to exist, and therefore there will be no future, only the present which will be the past in the future.

Woman: Did the book lie?

Man: Which one?

Woman: The one I had read long ago. Remember? I had told you about it, and about my escapades in the East.

Man: Ah yes, I remember. I am not familiar with that work I am afraid. I did say that I shall introduce myself to it. However, I think it is safe to conclude, despite being a preconceived conclusion, that it lied, as all books do.

Woman: Do they?

Man: Madam, human beings lie. Human beings are responsible for the books. Therefore, it follows that the books lie.

Woman: How thoughtless of me not to have thought that!

Man: It is quite easy to be so, especially when one is blinded by one's bias towards texts that one has studied. We like familiarity, it gives us comfort and confidence. That is, of course, till familiarity begins to breed contempt.

Woman: I can vouch for that! That is exactly what happened to me! Which is why I am here now.

Man: Every action, or lack thereof, has a subsequent consequence that becomes known to us only after we feel it...

Woman: (*interrupting*) Seeingly?

Man: ...by experiencing it. (*pausing*) I beg your pardon, I missed what you said. Would you be so kind as to repeat yourself?

Woman: Why?

Man:	What?
Woman:	They are just as good as one another.
Man:	Indeed, one is always as good as another. All other things being equal, one is always one, and another is another. One is, therefore, always the same as another.
Woman:	Why?
Man:	What?
Woman:	Either.
Man:	Or?
Woman:	(*looking up*) Rain?
Man:	It is not. (*looking down*) But will it?
Woman:	What do you think?
Man:	I cannot know for sure.
Adam:	(*interrupting*) How strong is our will?
Man:	(*turning to Adam for the first time*) What do you mean boy?
Adam:	Well sir…it's just that mother and I willed it not to rain…though it was a long time ago…well, some time ago at least. I don't know how strong our will is, so I don't know how long it will last…I'm sorry if I did wrong.
Man:	Put your mind at ease. Your mother led you, and you followed. Be it wrong or right, you had no way of knowing. However, your mother led, and you believed it to be right because of her status. She is an intelligent lady, and so she knew what she was doing. Put your mind at ease.
Adam:	(*relaxing*) I am happy to hear that!
Man:	And so you should be.
Woman:	(*turning to Adam*) Who is winning?
Adam:	I can't say for sure.
Woman:	That can't be very good.
Adam:	(*hangs his head in shame*) I am sorry mother.
Woman:	Nonsense! It only means that you can continue playing.
Adam:	(*smiling*) Thank you. (*begins playing with Eve again*)
Man:	So it could rain.
Woman:	Do you think so?
Man:	It is only reasonable for it to, at some point in time.
Woman:	Just as well! I am quite thirsty.
Man:	That is natural, the journey does that to you. That is why we make it.
Woman:	Poetic justice.
Man:	Poetry in motion.
Woman:	What were you saying?
Man:	I do not know.
Woman:	Oh, yes, I remember you saying that.
Man:	You follow me then?
Woman:	Always, till death.

Man:	Of course, but not beyond.
Woman:	I can't, beyond, can I?
Man:	You have come this far without missing a step, or taking a false step. You have done well thus far. Beyond that I cannot say for I do not know.
Woman:	Thank you for your kind words, you are as generous as you are wise.
Man:	Thank you madam.
Woman:	What shall we do now?
Man:	Wait the night out.
Woman:	Why?
Man:	What?
Woman:	Just as well.
Man:	Patience is a virtue.
Woman:	Then a doctor is needed.
Man:	And so I shall be.
Woman:	What?
Man:	Waiting, that is what I do, sometimes.

Enter the Knight noisily from right of stage. Adam and Eve stop playing. Eve looks up to see the Knight, Adam follows the noise made by the Knight's entrance. Eve then makes herself comfortable, curls up and goes to sleep. Adam feels for Eve, sees that she is asleep, and then curls up next to her and falls asleep. Knight follows all of their actions attentively, and then looks around, confused.

Knight:	I…forgive me, I must have taken a wrong turn somewhere.
Woman:	Are you the doctor?
Knight:	Which one?
Woman:	The one for the patients.
Knight:	Aren't they all?
Woman:	Yes. So you are the doctor?
Knight:	The doctor?
Woman:	Yes, a doctor.
Knight:	Oh no, I am not a doctor. You are as mistaken as I am! I am a knight.
Man:	Mistaken, sir? How so?
Knight:	Because I took a wrong turn.
Man:	(*looking around*) Where from? Wherefore?
Knight:	I'm sorry, but I don't know.
Man:	That is perfectly understandable.
Knight:	Thank you. (*looking around sheepishly*) There are no bushes here.
Woman:	Bushes? Why?
Knight:	(*alarmed*) So it is true, I did take a wrong turn!
Woman:	Why?

Knight:	(*turning to the Woman*) Oh, sorry, I got distracted. I was looking for bushes because I had to go. I must have taken a wrong turn somewhere along the line because otherwise I wouldn't have ended up here, where there are no bushes. And…(*pausing, turning to the Man; suddenly realisation dawns on him, and he takes a few steps back, almost walking off the stage*) Wait a minute, are you him? Or he? You must be!
Man:	Indeed I must, if you say I must.
Woman:	(*feeling herself, and then turning to the Man*) He must mean you, I don't fit the physical criteria to be him, or he. (*turning to the Knight*) Yes sir Knight, he must be.
Knight:	What good fortune! Such happy chance! Wait right here, I will be right back. (*runs off stage, using the exit to right of stage, then runs back in*) With my companions that is, the three of us, the venerable three. (*runs off the stage again, using the exit to right of stage, then runs back in*) A thousand apologies to the one, not venerable, for you are the revered one. (*runs off the stage again, using the exit to right of stage, then runs back in*) A thousand more apologies, I forgot to take my leave. (*bows*) I take my leave from you, the one. Please don't take any offence in my unbecoming actions. (*runs off the stage again, using the exit to right of stage, then runs back in*) A thousand more apologies, I forgot to inform you of your need to be here…
Man:	Do not fear, I shall be here, and so shall the three, for they travel with me.
Knight:	(*pausing*) But…forgive me, but I don't see the three.
Man:	(*pointing to the Woman, Adam and Eve*) There, behold, the three.
Knight:	I understand now, the three that travel with you.
Man:	Indeed.
Knight:	Then you will wait here?
Man:	Of course, I shall be waiting, that is what I do, sometimes.
Knight:	(*relieved and excited*) Excellent. You will wait here…with them of course…and I'll be right back, as fast as the road allows me.
Man:	Take your time, the road will be here, and so shall we.
Knight:	(*pausing*) Begging your pardon, but how will I find my way back?
Man:	The same way in which you found your way here the first time.
Knight:	But that was because I took a wrong turn.
Man:	Do not worry, all roads lead to the town, all except one.
Knight:	But we aren't in the town (*looking around*) are we?
Man:	Of course not, the town is that way (*pointing to the fork on the right in the background*), further along the road.
Knight:	So how will I find my way here.
Man:	You shall because all roads lead to the town, save one, (*pointing to the fork on the left in the background*) that one. That means that

	we are not on the only road that does not lead to the town. We are thus on the road to and from the town, and since all roads lead to the town, save that one which we are not on, you will find your way here, eventually. Simply follow the road, and you shall find your way.
Knight:	(*relieved*) This is good news indeed. So you will wait here?
Man:	Yes, I shall be waiting, that is what I do, sometimes.
Knight:	Excellent! I will be back along the road that will eventually lead me to here, and as a result to you. I will bring my companions who will be thrilled to meet you…meet him…or he. (*getting excited*) Oh happy chance! I take my leave from all, but only momentarily, only till I return with them to meet you, and him, or he. Till then.
Man:	I shall be waiting, that is what I do, sometimes.
Woman:	Travel safe!

Exit Knight to right of stage.

Woman:	What were you saying?
Man:	That I am waiting.
Woman:	Oh, of course. (*pauses*) What a nice gentleman!
Man:	Perfectly delightful.
Woman:	I have been blessed.
Man:	Indeed?
Woman:	Well, I must have been. I have met two nice gentlemen in a short space of time. Had I not married the first, I'd have been in a conundrum.
Man:	How so?
Woman:	You are both gentlemen, but I am this gentleman's wife, so the other's existence is immaterial for the faithful. Just as well, if his companions are gentlemen too, then my challenge would have been all the greater had I not married you. How then would I have picked one from so many?
Man:	Are you faithful though, madam?
Woman:	I can't say that I am faithless. I mean, I wouldn't say that I am, at least. Well, I may be going through a period of intense doubt, or confusion. That doesn't qualify as being faithless, does it?
Man:	Are you still honest with me?
Woman:	I am. But what does that have anything to do with anything?
Man:	If you are not dishonest with me, then you are not faithless, and therefore cannot say that you are. It turns out that you were correct the first time.
Woman:	So if I had to pick, I would have had to pick you in order to not be faithless?

Man:	Had you been faced with a choice of gentlemen, then it would have been a grave and daunting matter, for all gentlemen are equal, and as such, one gentleman is as good as another. I would have sympathised with your most grievous circumstances, until you had made a choice. Should you have overcome the unfair obstacle, with each singing praises of himself, preaching to a most attentive choir in you, it would indeed have been admirable. Had your struggles ended with you choosing me, then you would have been bound to being faithful to me. Adultery, emotional or physical, would not have been tolerated, unless it had been preceded by a complete divorce, of thought, of conscience, of everything, for then it would not have been adultery at all, rather an alteration of faith that would have annulled any preconceived notions of faithlessness on your part. Faithfulness, after all, begins in faithlessness.
Woman:	So it wouldn't matter if I am faithless?
Man:	It is irrelevant. The entire question, or questioning, of your faith is immaterial because all of it was based on a hypothetical situation that did not come to pass to any extent.
Woman:	So my faith doesn't matter?
Man:	Given how things have come to pass, I would have to say that no, it does not.
Woman:	Well, am I faithful then?
Man:	Since you did not have to choose by selecting before being presented with all the choices, and then decided to stay true to your preference, it would appear that you are, and have remained, faithful. As I have said, however, it is all irrelevant, immaterial.
Woman:	Oh, what a relief! I am relieved!
Man:	Perhaps that is why he was looking for a bush.
Woman:	Who? Why?
Man:	The Knight, to relieve himself.
Woman:	Why?
Man:	When nature calls, you must answer, as you have so intelligently displayed.
Woman:	But nature has not called me.
Man:	Forgive me madam, I was under the impression that it had, and that you had devised a new method of relieving yourself without requiring the assistance of a bush.
Woman:	Isn't that the sort of thing that happens in Sanctuary?
Man:	I understand that it used to happen till food was served for the first time. Then again, it is a mental asylum after all, so it could still happen, for such things are known to happen in such places.
Woman:	You are right!
Man:	You know, then?
Woman:	Know what?

Man:	What you claim to know.
Woman:	But I do not know anything, because no-one knows anything.
Man:	Then you do not know that I am right.
Woman:	You are very intelligent, sir, that is what attracted me to you. It was intoxicating enough to make me want to sin, if one can sin that is. You can't be wrong because you are definitely intelligent…
Man:	And so I must be right? I cannot say that I can fault your logic, it seems impeccable.
Woman:	Impregnable, which is why it does not exist.
Man:	It does not exist because it does not live, and it is not alive because it does not exist. Unlike it, the Knight does exist.
Woman:	But his existence is immaterial to the faithful, and since I am faithful, his existence is immaterial.
Man:	He exists, therefore he is, and hence he lives. It cannot be immaterial, existence can never be immaterial. Irrelevant it can be, and at times is, but immaterial it cannot.
Woman:	Does that change my faithfulness?
Man:	That, madam, is irrelevant.
Woman:	Still so?
Man:	Indeed.
Woman:	Oh, what a relief! I am relieved.
Man:	If you say so, it would appear so.
Woman:	So what about the Knight's existence?
Man:	What of it?
Woman:	What does it mean?
Man:	It means that he is, and that he lives.
Woman:	But how does that change anything? Does it change anything?
Man:	It changes nothing.
Woman:	Why not?
Man:	Because he wants us to wait here for him to return with his companions.
Woman:	I see. We were going to wait even if he hadn't wanted us to?
Man:	Yes, I would have, and so you would have for you know not the road ahead.
Woman:	That is true! (*looking around, her eyesight catching a glimpse of Adam and Eve*) The children are asleep.
Man:	Children have a lower level of stamina and tolerance, which makes them grow tired easily.
Woman:	Not weary?
Man:	No, that is an adult concoction, a figment of the adult's imagination that has crept into reality. No, not weary. They are tired, and hence they sleep.
Woman:	(*yawning*) I am tired too.
Man:	You would be, you have been up for longer than the boy and the girl.

Woman:	I too shall sleep then.
Man:	That would be the natural result of, and logical solution to, being tired.
Woman:	(*lying down*) What will you do?
Man:	I shall wait, that is what I do, sometimes.

The Woman falls asleep. The Man continues to sit and wait. It is completely dark by now, because it is deep in the night.

End of Act.

Act 3

ACT 3 Scene 1

The Woman, Adam and Eve are asleep in the middle of the stage. The man is sitting to the left of the stage, staring straight at the audience and deep in thought. The backdrop is as it previously was, with two paths, a fork in the road: the one on the right is descending, and is lush, rich and full of life, while the one on the left is ascending, and is barren, overcast and surrounded by death. It is still dark. [The man is expressionless at all times. It is completely dark, deep in the night, with morning some way away]

Man: (*expressionless, motionless, deep in thought, continues to stare at the audience, then suddenly looks away as if waking up from a trance*) Curious, very curious. A dreaming reality without really dreaming. A vision perhaps, but I cannot lay claims to such wisdom. (*stands up and stretches without making any noise*) Drinking some water is what needs doing I think, for my solace is to be the quenching of thirst. Unless that brings contemplation to an end, in which case it is best avoided. (*looking up at the sky*) Still no sign of rain, which is disconcerting. However, it is difficult to tell through the darkness. That is perhaps for the best, I can rest easy knowing that the grave predicament presented by the whole business of quenching has been averted, at least temporarily. Except I am waiting, and hence not resting. (*turns slowly to look at the Woman, Adam and Eve, examines them intently, then looks at the backdrop thoughtfully, and finally turns back to face the audience*) They sleep. That is for the best. The road ahead is long, and so they must be well-rested. It was foretold as I was waiting that we know not what road is to be our destiny despite the destination always having been the same. Regardless, it will be long, and so rest is essential. (*walks towards the edge of the stage*) Our company is lighter than it is meant to be, but…(*looking up*)…yes there is no way of telling how long has passed. It is too dark for that too.

Enter Advisor from right of stage.

Man: (*without turning to see the Advisor, still looking up and examining*) Who walks there?
Advisor: I come in peace, and we come in pieces.
Man: (*turning towards the Advisor*) I observe the peace, but see no pieces.

Advisor:	(*looking over his shoulder*) I was closely followed by the rest of my party.
Man:	You led them here?
Advisor:	No, I was led here.
Man:	Then you followed.
Advisor:	No, I was followed.
Man:	Then you must have led.
Advisor:	No, I could not have led as I knew not the way.
Man:	Then you followed.
Advisor:	You would appear to be right.
Man:	Did you lose your party?
Advisor:	It would appear I did.
Man:	So you could be in the wrong place?
Advisor:	I could, but I was assured of company by one in my company.
Man:	There is no other on the road?
Advisor:	None besides the ones I travel with.
Man:	Would they be the same ones that you have misplaced?
Advisor:	Yes, that would be correct.
Man:	One of them promised you company?
Advisor:	Yes, he did.
Man:	Could he not have lied?
Advisor:	(*calmly*) No sir, he could not, it is not his disposition to do so because he is unable to do so, as it goes against what he is.
Man:	I believe you, but you could still be in the wrong place.
Advisor:	Our long travels yielded no other life, yours being the first. I would say that I may not be in the wrong place.
Man:	You are, however, lost?
Advisor:	No, I was directed to come this way by the one who informed us all about the company.
Man:	Your company is not here.
Advisor:	(*impressed*) Well observed!
Man:	So you are lost.
Advisor:	You would appear to be right.
Man:	I think it best you wait with me. You were led here by the one who instructed you. He was one of the company who followed behind you. You were promised company, and I could be he. You are lost, but you may be found. Then the whole thing will come to light. I suggest you wait.
Advisor:	(*realisation dawning on him*) Yes, yes, I remember being told that he, or him, would be there, or here.
Man:	I fit the description.
Advisor:	Loosely speaking, we all do.
Man:	Almost all of us.
Advisor:	Of course, of course.
Man:	So you shall wait with me?

Advisor:	Till I am found?
Man:	And till it is all made clear?
Advisor:	So that we can then continue on our journey?
Man:	Should our destination be the same?
Advisor:	Or for as long as our paths coincide?
Man:	We are decided then?
Advisor:	Are we meant to be?
Man:	What do you think?
Advisor:	Am I to think?
Man:	Are you?
Advisor:	I am, therefore I think, correct?
Man:	You think you think, or you think?
Advisor:	About what?
Man:	What do you think?

Enter Knight from right of stage, short of breath.

Knight:	(*panting*) A thousand apologies and more!
Advisor:	I am found!
Man:	(*looking away nonchalantly*) I thought you would return.
Knight:	(*prostrating to catch his breath*) He is him, or he.
Man:	Is he now? I thought you were bringing more?
Advisor:	He is? That will require due consideration before a decision is made and a judgment is passed.
Knight:	(*standing up again and looking around*) They were right behind me.
Man:	No, he was in front of you.
Advisor:	Where are they now? Where did you last see them?
Knight:	(*pointing to the Advisor*) He was in front of me, but (*pointing towards the exit on right on stage*) they were behind me, at least… (*looking sheepish and ashamed*)…till I stopped to do what one must so as to avoid any accidents. Just as I was about to relieve myself, I noticed that you were not there, so I began to search for you frantically.
Advisor:	Yes, I was not there, because I was here. You searched, and you found, which is why I am not lost anymore.
Man:	(*still looking away*) Yes, he was here, I can vouch for that, which is why he was not there. I was here too, and now, since you are here, he is found, and you found your way back.
Knight:	(*to the Man*) I would have lost myself had you not told me about all the roads leading to the town.
Man:	Nonsense. You would still have found your way back without losing yourself because even had you not known about the fact that all the roads lead to the town, that fact would still have

	remained. You would thus have found your way back here, as long as you were not on that road (*gesturing towards the fork on the left in the background*), the only one that leads elsewhere and not to the town.
Advisor:	(*following the man's gesture*) Yes, of course, the fork in the road and he, or him, by it. (*things begin to make sense to him*) So we are here. That is good news.
Knight:	Good news indeed.
Advisor:	(*to the Knight*) It would be even better news had we all been here. Then it would be great news.
Knight:	I shall go look for them to make this great news.
Man:	(*still looking away*) What if they are looking for you?
Knight:	What then?
Man:	Would it not be wise for you to wait here and be found?
Knight:	Am I wise?
Man:	You will be if you do what has been proven to be successful in the past.
Knight:	I would like that very much, it would please me.
Man:	Then wait here as our common acquaintance did in order to cease to be lost by being found by you. These others that you speak of will follow suit and relieve you of your burden, and your company will then be complete.
Advisor:	Then we will all be here, and this will be great news. (*to the Man*) Sir, you are as wise as you are kind. Very uncommon…(*thinking deeply*)…yes, very uncommon for the common, which would be ideal for him, or he. The case grows stronger.
Knight:	It would be uncommonly good to finally be able to relieve myself. I have been made to hold back for far too long, since coming of age. It is certain to effect my health.
Man:	Then wait with us.
Knight:	I shall!
Advisor:	It is decided then.

The three of them turn towards the audience and prepare to sit and wait. Just then, the Doctor and the Jester enter from right of stage, then pause and hesitate.

Man:	(*sitting down, not turning to see the Doctor and the Jester, instead looking at the audience*) Who comes?
Knight:	Not I.
Advisor:	Nor I. It would be physically impossible to do so once I have already done so. (*checks to see that what he said is right, and then, content that it is, sits down. He proceeds to check the exits to see who has entered, and then follows them with his eyes closely and intently*)

Knight:	I wouldn't know.
Doctor:	(*to the Jester*) Familiar voices, I shall announce ourselves.
Jester:	(*to the Doctor*) No-one likes repetition.
Doctor:	What do you mean?
Jester:	You announced us by announcing that you'll announce us.
Doctor:	I didn't mention you.
Jester:	You did, by mentioning "us".
Doctor:	But that may not have specifically referred to you.
Jester:	It did though, didn't it?
Doctor:	Yes.
Jester:	Then you announced us, and now you're being redundant.
Doctor:	I wasn't made redundant, I made myself so.
Jester:	Stop deflecting. You are being repetitive, and no-one likes it.
Doctor:	I'm sorry.
Jester:	You should be.
Doctor:	I am.
Jester:	Good.
Knight:	(*silently sneaking up beside the Jester and the Doctor*) No, great! Friends! This is great news!
Doctor:	(*noticing the Knight and embracing him*) Friend! We found you!
Jester:	(*startled by the sudden intrusion*) Who? What? (*relieved after seeing the Knight*) Ah, it is you, you, forever you. How do you mean? (*waiting for an answer as the two embrace, getting slightly agitated*) Are you quite done with your over-exuberance? People will start thinking ill of you because of that. (*getting more annoyed because the two still embrace*) Yes, yes, that'll do. Answer me now! (*no response*) Well, take your time then. It isn't as if we have any reason to hurry. After all, we haven't really been travelling for an eternity to humour someone's stupidity.
Doctor:	(*finally remembering the Jester and breaking off from the embrace*) Oh, forgive me.
Jester:	For what?
Doctor:	For that.
Jester:	For that? There isn't anything I can do about it. Most I can do is take offence, but since I'm open-minded, I have no problems with it. Whatever floats your boat.
Doctor:	Thank you, that relieves me.
Knight:	I wish it had the same effect on me. I wish so hard to be relieved.
Jester:	He speaks! Now answer me.
Knight:	(*to the Jester*) I have been rude to you I realise. Let me make it up to you. What can I do?
Jester:	You can answer me!
Knight:	What is your question?

Jester:	(*turning to the Doctor, exasperated*) What is my question he asks me, what is my question! Tell him!
Doctor:	Tell him what?
Jester:	(*getting angry*) My question!
Doctor:	Which one?
Jester:	The important one that I asked him before the two of you decided to indulge yourselves.
Doctor:	Oh, that one. Yes, you must be answered. (*to the Knight*) He must be answered.
Jester:	(*calming down*) Finally, someone sees sense. Thank you. (*turning back to the Knight*) So, answer me.
Knight:	I shall.
Jester:	Get on with it then, we haven't got all day.
Knight:	Yes.
Jester:	Yes what?
Knight:	Just yes.
Jester:	That's it? Just yes? What kind of an answer is that?
Doctor:	(*to the Jester*) If I may intervene…
Jester:	Unless you have the answer, this does not concern you.
Doctor:	But you didn't ask me, so I can't possibly have the answer.
Jester:	Then stay out of this.
Doctor:	As you please. (*takes a few steps away from the Jester and the Knight*)
Knight:	Yes.
Jester:	I heard you the first time you incorrigible waste! Answer me!
Knight:	A new question?
Jester:	Why should it be a new question when you never answered the first one?
Knight:	How do you mean?
Jester:	What do you mean?
Knight:	I don't have a meaning.
Jester:	Then why didn't you just say that in the first place?
Knight:	I didn't know I was supposed to.
Jester:	Why wouldn't you know that?
Knight:	I don't know.
Doctor:	(*interrupting from a distance*) If I may make an observation…
Jester:	(*turning towards the Doctor*) Is it going to be constructive?
Doctor:	I don't know.
Jester:	(*frustrated*) You don't know, he doesn't know, nobody knows.
Knight:	That seems to be the case.
Jester:	(*turning back to the Knight*) So why didn't you say so in the first place?
Knight:	(*becoming happy*) Another question! I'll make it up to you now by answering.
Jester:	Humour me.

Knight: I…What was the question again?
Jester: Why didn't you say so in the first place?
Knight: I don't know.
Jester: (*very frustrated*) I give up.
Doctor: Let me clarify.
Jester: (*to the Doctor*) Can you?
Doctor: Was that a question?
Jester: Yes, it was.
Doctor: Then I'll answer it.
Jester: No, you really don't have to.
Knight: Friends! This is great! This is great news!
Jester: What is?
Knight: You are here!
Doctor: Yes! We are!
Jester: Yes, no thanks to you.
Knight: (*hanging his head in shame*) I'm sorry.
Jester: You should be.
Knight: I am.
Jester: Good.
Doctor: He didn't mean it.
Jester: Shut up!
Knight: I didn't?
Doctor: (*walking towards the Knight*) Of course you didn't! You had to relieve yourself.
Jester: (*turning towards the Knight*) Oh yes, how did that go?
Knight: Dreadfully. I failed.
Jester: (*knowingly*) Of course you did.
Doctor: (*consoling the Knight*) Don't be disheartened. I'll help you with it.
Knight: That is very kind of you.
Jester: So, what happened this time?
Knight: Just as I was about to, I noticed that sir Advisor was missing, so I rushed to find him.
Jester: And did you?
Knight: Yes, I did.
Doctor: This is great news!
Knight: But then I lost you.
Jester: (*sarcastically*) Did you now?
Doctor: Yes, he did.
Knight: But now that you've found me, we're all here, and this is great news!
Advisor: (*remaining seated*) Yes, this is great news. He is very wise indeed, he foretold all of this.
Jester: (*turning towards the Advisor*) Who? He? And why didn't you intervene earlier?

Advisor:	You did not want my intervention.	
Doctor:	That is true, you didn't want his or mine.	
Jester:	(*to the Doctor and the Knight*) Your combined idiocy knows no bounds. Inability to procreate because of your evils means that there is some good to come of it. (*the Doctor and the Knight hang their heads in shame*) Now…(*turning back to the Advisor*)…you have my complete and undivided attention. You were saying?	
Advisor:	No, you were asking.	
Jester:	Yes, I was, and then you were saying.	
Advisor:	Yes, that is correct.	
Jester:	Are you done saying?	
Advisor:	I do not think I answered you entirely.	
Jester:	I believe you.	
Advisor:	Thank you.	
Jester:	(*walking towards the Advisor*) So, you were saying?	
Advisor:	Yes, this here (*pointing to the Man*) sitting beside me is he.	
Knight:	I said as much to you before! I was right!	
Doctor:	Friend!	
Jester:	(*recognising the Man and becoming angry*) You!	
Man:	(*still looking at the audience*) Yes.	
Jester:	You are he? (*to the Advisor, completely shocked*) He is he?	
Advisor:	I do not have an answer to that question.	
Doctor:	(*to the Advisor, earnestly*) He can't be. He told me he wasn't.	
Man:	(*turning to the others*) Did I?	
Knight:	(*to the Doctor*) He did? When?	
Doctor:	When I met him.	
Knight:	You have met before?	
Man:	Not once, but twice before. Our third meeting marks his second coming.	
Knight:	(*to the Doctor*) You must teach me your remarkable skills.	
Doctor:	I'll do all I can friend, for you, for friendship.	
Knight:	Thank you.	
Jester:	(*regaining composure and turning to the Advisor*) So is he or is he not he?	
Advisor:	That will require due consideration before a decision is made and a judgment is passed.	
Jester:	What will you need to make that happen?	
Advisor:	Some peace.	
Jester:	You shall have it. Anything else that I can do to aid expediency?	
Advisor:	Nothing that I can think of right now.	
Jester:	Alright. (*turning to the Doctor and the Knight*) This is where the two of you follow me.	
Doctor:	Why?	
Knight:	(*to the Jester*) Where are we going? (*to the Doctor*) I do like travelling! It's so liberating!	

Jester:	(*turning towards the exit to right of stage and beginning to walk towards it*) Away from here, because we need to give him some peace.
Knight:	So he is him, or he! I was right!
Doctor:	But I thought that he wasn't?
Jester:	(*turning towards the Knight and the Doctor, slightly irritated*) We don't know! Weren't you listening? The Advisor needs some peace to know, so let us give that to him. (*turning back towards the exit*) Now, follow me.
Doctor:	Certainly!
Knight:	You lead, and I follow.

Exit Jester, Doctor and Knight to right of stage, the Jester leading and the other two following.

Man:	(*to the Advisor*) Were they not your companions?
Advisor:	Yes.
Man:	So they found you?
Advisor:	Yes.
Man:	That is good.
Advisor:	You knew they would.
Man:	I said so by using logic and deduction.
Advisor:	And you were right.
Man:	It would appear so.
Advisor:	You are uncommonly wise.
Man:	I shall have to believe you.
Advisor:	What shall we do now?
Man:	(*looking away*) I shall wait, that is what I do, sometimes.
Advisor:	Remarkable! Magnificent! I shall follow suit.

Silence. The two wait. After a while, the Jester returns, hurriedly entering from right of stage.

Jester:	(*visibly impatient*) Are you done? I grow impatient.
Advisor:	Do not interrupt him, he waits.
Jester:	(*to the Advisor*) So he is him, or he?
Advisor:	That will require due consideration before a decision is made and a judgment is passed.
Jester:	Yes, and you needed peace to come to a conclusion.
Advisor:	Where are the others?
Jester:	(*disgusted*) They were merry when they remembered finding one another, so I left them to embrace.
Advisor:	Does that make you uneasy?

Jester:	(*shrugging*) No, but I tried explaining to them that some might not take too kindly to it.
Advisor:	That is true.
Jester:	Yes, but the fools wouldn't listen.
Advisor:	Most unsatisfactory, most unfortunate.
Jester:	For them, yes. Perhaps you could tell them? They put more stock in your words.
Advisor:	I shall if you think it best.
Jester:	It's worth a try.
Advisor:	Very well, I shall oblige. Bring them to me.
Jester:	Alright.

Exit Jester to right of stage.

Man:	(*turning to the Advisor*) Are they not satisfied to have found you?
Advisor:	(*turning to face the Man*) Should they be?
Man:	Seeing as they are your companions, it is only natural.
Advisor:	Relieved perhaps, true.
Man:	I would not know about that, nor can I pretend to.
Advisor:	That is singular sir! I thought I was the only celibate one.
Man:	I do not believe celibacy has anything to do with being lost.
Advisor:	I cannot say I know of any correlation.
Man:	They still seem lost.
Advisor:	Are not all of us so?
Man:	Not I, nor my company. We know our destiny, and fate has it that we now stand on its threshold.
Advisor:	The more you speak, the more I begin to be convinced of my companions and I being united with our destiny, our fate.
Man:	It is very fulfilling.
Advisor:	I certainly hope so.
Man:	You should know so, for knowing reaches beyond feeble faith.
Advisor:	Truer words have seldom been spoken.
Man:	You are uniquely kind.
Advisor:	"Do unto others as you would have others do unto you." You seem to live by the same maxim.
Man:	I am but a peaceful, docile being. I am yet to be given a reason to be otherwise.
Advisor:	You speak as I would! We seem to be cut from the same cloth…
Man:	(*turning away*) There is no evidence to prove or disprove that.
Advisor:	…except that you seem to be the master of what I am merely a pupil.
Man:	Hardly sir, the self-serving nature of self-deprecation does not beget you.
Advisor:	Created in your image perhaps?

Man:	I would know of my own image had I given way to vanity.
Advisor:	Is it lack of vanity, or lack of a medium of reflection, that prevents you from knowing of your image?
Man:	A plethora of reflecting media abound all around us. Lack of vanity it is, I am sure of it, for I have no reason to give in to it.
Advisor:	I test you, and you pass the test by testing me in turn with a riddle! You could be he, or him! Regretfully, I have no answer to your riddle.
Man:	Is there a riddle to be solved? Of course there is, it is that of existence.
Advisor:	I have every reason to believe you.
Man:	(*turning back to the Advisor*) Are your companions to return?
Advisor:	If my memory serves me right, yes, they are to return.
Man:	They all seem so familiar, all but yourself.
Advisor:	I am hardly the enigma that your statement suggests. Unfamiliar with you, however, I am, most unfortunately.
Man:	Unfortunately for me, yes.
Advisor:	Perish the thought, I meant for myself sir! It could never be unfortunate for you! For myself on the other hand, yes, it is indeed very unfortunate. Even more so if what you say is true, that I should be the last to meet you.
Man:	Of that I am certain.
Advisor:	(*gravely*) Then it is most unfortunate. Things could have been so different had we met sooner.
Man:	Everything affects everything, causal nexus, yes. You are too kind sir.
Advisor:	Thank you sir, thank you. (*looks around, worried*)
Man:	Is something the matter?
Advisor:	I grow concerned for my companions, my friends.
Man:	Is there something I can do to ease your anxiety?
Advisor:	I am not deserving of such kindness sir. (*getting up*) I should search for them.
Man:	(*turning away*) That would serve no point or purpose.
Advisor:	How so?
Man:	They know where you are, while you do not know where they are. They are to return, while you were never to go where they are. They are to be here, while you were never to be where they are.
Advisor:	I cannot refute any of that, but I still worry. Call it an old man's curse, but the distress I feel grows.
Man:	That is understandable, and dispel it you must.
Advisor:	Then you shall understand if I were to leave you for a brief while?
Man:	So you intend to search for them?
Advisor:	I feel I must.

Man:	(*turning back to the Advisor*) If that is to be the case, then…(*getting up*)…let me go in your stead.
Advisor:	I could not allow that to happen!
Man:	You have journeyed far and long, you are tired. Stay here and rest a while, in peace. I shall aid by doing what you feel you must.
Advisor:	An act too generous for my meagre gratefulness.
Man:	Nonsense.
Advisor:	Do you remember which direction they went?
Man:	I do indeed, though retracing their footsteps in this darkness may prove to be arduous.
Advisor:	Do you want to wait for the light?
Man:	I shall continue to do that, but after I have found your companions and brought them back.
Advisor:	We are decided then?
Man:	We have always been.
Advisor:	I shall be here.
Man:	You shall, you shall.

Man begins to move towards the exit to right of stage. Just then, the Knight enters from right of stage.

Knight:	I was summoned.
Man:	So you have returned.
Knight:	I have for I was summoned, or so said the one that went to fetch us.
Advisor:	(*moving towards right of stage to meet the Knight*) Greetings! And where is he?
Knight:	He is right…(*turns around*)…right…(*looks around*)…well…(*perplexed*)…I don't know.
Advisor:	And the other?
Knight:	He is right…(*turns around*)…right…(*looks around*)…well…(*perplexed*)…I don't know.
Man:	(*to the Advisor*) Should I continue?
Advisor:	Would that be wise?
Man:	Does he know whether they are on their way?
Advisor:	(*to the Knight*) Are they on their way?
Knight:	On their way here you mean?
Advisor:	(*to the Man*) On their way here you mean?
Man:	Yes, that is implied.
Advisor:	(*to the Knight*) Yes, that is implied.
Knight:	They were, that is to say they are.
Advisor:	(*to the Man*) They were, that is to say they are.
Man:	Then they shall be here.
Advisor:	It would appear so.

Man:	In that case, I do not think it would be wise to search for them, since they are on their way here.
Advisor:	I am inclined to agree with you.
Knight:	(*still perplexed, searching around the stage*) I could have sworn they were with me. By that logic, they should be here, but I can't see them anywhere, nor can I find them here. This is most unsettling, very disturbing!
Advisor:	(*to the Knight*) Do not concern yourself, everything is alright.
Knight:	Is it?
Advisor:	Yes, we are decided.
Knight:	When did that happen?
Man:	(*to the Knight*) We have always been.
Knight:	That is good news!
Advisor:	No, that is great news!
Knight:	Why great news?
Advisor:	Because I did not know until it was pointed out to me.
Man:	(*to the Advisor*) But the fact that you did not know did not change the fact that the fact existed, and remained.
Advisor:	That is true, but since I did not know, I could not celebrate it.
Knight:	Which is why it is great news?
Advisor:	Indeed!
Man:	It seems to have reached a satisfactory conclusion then?
Advisor:	The conclusion is still to be had.
Knight:	Or heard.
Advisor:	Or seen.
Knight:	Or smelt.
Advisor:	Or felt.
Knight:	Or tasted.
Advisor:	Or decided.
Knight:	But I thought you have always been decided?
Man:	Yes, we have.
Knight:	Then the conclusion can't be yet to be decided.
Man:	We are decided, we have always been. The conclusion, however, unlike us, is not and has not been, yet.
Advisor:	Indeed.
Knight:	I think I understand.
Advisor:	Which one?
Knight:	Which one out of what?
Advisor:	The two you mentioned.
Knight:	My memory has never been my strength, I don't remember mentioning two.
Man:	A sharp wit is not necessarily a strength if not applied correctly, or harnessed. You are better than you think yourself to be.
Knight:	You are right! Thank you friend!
Advisor:	Think it is then. Good.

Knight:	No, great!
Man:	Indeed.
Advisor:	So where are the others?
Knight:	(*panicking*) Forgive me, please, I don't know! Forgive me! They are not here! Forgive me! They are lost! Forgive me! I am lost!
Advisor:	(*looking down*) We all are…
Man:	Calm yourself, everything is alright.
Advisor:	Except him. He cannot be, for he is the shepherd.
Knight:	(*calming down*) I trust you, you have always been right.
Advisor:	(*looking up at the Man and the Knight again*) So I hope.
Man:	So I am told.
Knight:	(*hesitating*) I…
Advisor:	Yes?
Knight:	(*unsure*) I…
Advisor:	Yes?
Knight:	(*hesitating and unsure*) I…need to relieve myself.
Man:	A man must do what a man must do.
Advisor:	Did you encounter any bushes on your way after being summoned?
Knight:	I didn't, which is why I haven't, yet.
Man:	(*pointing to the left of stage*) Try that way, there may be something there.
Knight:	Thank you, I will. Please wait for me.
Advisor:	Do not worry, take your time.
Knight:	Thank you.

Exit Knight to left of stage.

Advisor:	I hope he succeeds this time.
Man:	(*turning to the Advisor*) It troubles him?
Advisor:	It seems to.
Man:	But it does not trouble you.
Advisor:	(*turning to the Man*) About myself or about him?
Man:	What does not trouble you?
Advisor:	My condition.
Man:	But his troubles you?
Advisor:	He is my companion, and a friend. It troubles me that he is troubled.
Man:	That is natural, and understandable. (*moves back to left of stage*)
Advisor:	Are you leaving too?
Man:	No, I would not, not without my companions.
Advisor:	That is very kind of you.
Man:	I will take your word for it.
Advisor:	So what is it that you do?

Man:	(*sitting down*) I wait, that is what I do, sometimes.
Advisor:	Forgive me for the misunderstanding, I shall phrase my question better. What is it that you are doing, or are about to do?
Man:	I am waiting, that is what I do, sometimes.
Advisor:	Most wise! I shall follow suit. (*sits down on right of stage*)

Enter Doctor from right of stage

Advisor:	(*looks up and at the Doctor*) So you are back.
Doctor:	(*looks down and around, sees the Advisor and looks at him*) I am, but I still don't know why it is we left, nor why I return.
Advisor:	Are you alone?
Doctor:	Not anymore, now that you are here.
Advisor:	I am not alone.
Doctor:	Of course you aren't, now that I am here.
Advisor:	I was not, even before you arrived.
Doctor:	Why was I made to leave?
Advisor:	You were not alone in that predicament.
Doctor:	That is true. Why were we made to leave?
Advisor:	Because I needed some peace for due consideration before a decision was made and a judgment was passed.
Doctor:	Oh yes, of course, I remember now. The Jester said so.
Advisor:	I believe he repeated what I had said to him, yes. Where is he?
Doctor:	(*looking up*) Isn't he here?
Advisor:	He was, but then he left to fetch the two of you so that I may enlighten you on the subject of prejudice.
Doctor:	I see. (*looking back down at the Advisor*) So, where is he?
Advisor:	I have not known of his location since he left us to seek you.
Doctor:	He told us to come this way, and said that he would shortly follow once he tended to some pressing business matter.
Advisor:	He has not deserted his job, nor shunned his duty then. That is good to know.
Doctor:	You have considered duly?
Advisor:	(*nodding his head*) As duly as I am able to consider for now. How did you know?
Doctor:	I supposed, because I am here, and you haven't asked me to leave.
Advisor:	(*impressed*) Your powers of deduction are sharp!
Doctor:	Thank you, I have had time to hone them on my long, lone journey. Are you decided?
Advisor:	We have always been.
Doctor:	(*confused*) Why, then, did you send us away?
Advisor:	Because I was not aware of the fact that we had always been decided.

Doctor:	But you know now?
Advisor:	I do not know.
Doctor:	(*confused*) You just said that you knew.
Advisor:	I believe what I said was that we have always been decided.
Doctor:	Yes, and then you said that you were not aware of that fact.
Advisor:	That is correct.
Doctor:	(*seeming to understand*) Ah, things are clearer now. You don't know, and you weren't aware.
Advisor:	That is correct.
Doctor:	Are you aware now?
Advisor:	Yes, I have been made aware recently.
Doctor:	Excellent! Has a judgment been passed?
Advisor:	No, it has not.
Doctor:	Why not?
Advisor:	Because we have not reached the conclusion.
Doctor:	That has not been decided?
Advisor:	We have always been decided, but the conclusion has not.
Doctor:	I don't understand.
Advisor:	Neither do I, but it is as it should be.
Doctor:	What do you mean?
Advisor:	(*deep in thought, looking down as if in a trance*) The judgment and the conclusion are intertwined. I could not have known that without your help, although I am certain that he knew…
Doctor:	He is he, or him?
Advisor:	…yes, he must have known. That is what the riddle must have meant. Either the judgment would lead to the conclusion being decided, or the conclusion would lead to the judgment being decided.
Doctor:	I think I follow. But he can't be he, or him, he told me he wasn't.
Advisor:	That may or may not be the case.
Doctor:	So he could be he, or him?
Advisor:	Anyone could be he or him.
Doctor:	Not everyone.
Advisor:	No, but anyone could.
Doctor:	Anyone could.
Advisor:	(*looking up at the Doctor again, as if breaking out of a trance*) Where are the others?
Doctor:	The others? Of whom do you speak?
Advisor:	Our companions.
Doctor:	New, or old?
Advisor:	Old to me, new to you.
Doctor:	The one you sent to fetch us is tending to some pressing business matter that I don't know anything else about, while my friend strode on ahead towards you, eager to hear what you had to say.

Advisor:	Then he would not have been best pleased.
Doctor:	Why not?
Advisor:	No-one likes being told about prejudices, they are an ugly business.
Doctor:	That is what I told the fool when he tried telling us about them!
Advisor:	Nevertheless, they need to be made known, and you need to be made aware of them.
Doctor:	Why?
Advisor:	Because that is the way it is, sadly.
Doctor:	I see.
Advisor:	Do you understand?
Doctor:	About the prejudices?
Advisor:	Yes.
Doctor:	Yes, I do.
Advisor:	And the causes and consequences of your actions?
Doctor:	(*shameful*) Yes.
Advisor:	And of misperceptions, misconceptions, misinterpretations and misunderstandings?
Doctor:	(*still shameful*) Yes, yes, yes and yes.
Advisor:	Then all is well.
Doctor:	I am relieved to hear that!
Advisor:	You relieve easily. That is what your friend is currently trying to do.
Doctor:	Which friend?
Advisor:	Your friend.
Doctor:	I have many.
Advisor:	Your friend, the one who strode on ahead towards us, eager to hear what I had to say.
Doctor:	Ah, yes, of course, it had to be him. He needed my help, my skills would have eased his burden.
Advisor:	His burden is great indeed.
Doctor:	I must go help him at once!
Advisor:	If you think you must.
Doctor:	Is it going to be alright if I leave you alone for some time?
Advisor:	I am not alone.
Doctor:	Good. Then it is alright if I leave?
Advisor:	As long as you know where you go.
Doctor:	Where do I go?
Advisor:	You know that better than I do.
Doctor:	Oh, yes, of course, towards my friend.
Advisor:	Which one?
Doctor:	The one who strode ahead towards you.
Advisor:	Not me?
Doctor:	No, I already know where you are, I wouldn't need to leave to go to you.

Advisor:	Well said! Not the other either?
Doctor:	Who is the other?
Advisor:	Either way, you shall find both if you travel in that (*pointing to the exit to left of stage*) direction.
Doctor:	Yes, yes, of course, yes, thank you.
Advisor:	Not at all.
Doctor:	(*moving towards the exit to left of stage*) I will return soon.
Advisor:	With your friend I presume?
Doctor:	Yes, as soon as I am able to help him with his problem.
Advisor:	Or sooner?
Doctor:	Yes, if you think that is best.
Advisor:	I do.

Doctor stumbles into the Man and almost falls over. The Man rises quickly and calmly, keeps him from falling over, and helps him regain his balance.

Doctor:	I'm so sorry, I didn't see you there!
Man:	My fault entirely for not making my presence known.
Doctor:	Thank you for helping me in my time of need, it wouldn't be the first time that you have done so.
Man:	Think nothing of it.
Doctor:	What were you doing here?
Man:	I was waiting, that is what I do, sometimes.
Doctor:	Of course you were, of course you were.
Man:	Are you leaving already?
Doctor:	I'm afraid I am.
Man:	So soon after your arrival?
Doctor:	I actually arrived some time ago. I was standing over there (*pointing to the spot where he was standing*) and conversing with him (*pointing at the Advisor*). Except he seems to have fallen asleep now.
Man:	He should sleep, and so should you. You have both travelled long and far.
Doctor:	Yes, I am beginning to feel tired. But I must go.
Man:	If you think you must.
Doctor:	Yes, I must. (*starts to walk towards the exit to left of stage again, then stops abruptly and turns around*) Wait, don't you want to know where I am going, or how long I'll be gone for?
Man:	If you wish to tell me, I shall not object.
Doctor:	It's the least I can do, after all you've done for me. I won't be gone for long.
Man:	I did not think you would be.
Doctor:	Why not?

Man:	Because this is where we are, and where you were meant to return to, and where you are meant to be.
Doctor:	Quite true. Well, I'll get going then. (*starts to walk towards the exit to left of stage again, then stops abruptly and turns around*) Wait, I almost forgot to tell you where I am going!
Man:	It would appear so.
Doctor:	Thank you for reminding me!
Man:	I am glad I could be of some assistance.
Doctor:	I am going to find my friend, help him with his troubles, and then return with him.
Man:	Most noble of intentions.
Doctor:	That is what friends are for, I think.
Man:	You are a good friend.
Doctor:	As are you.
Man:	So you tell me.
Doctor:	I'll go now.
Man:	All things being equal, we shall see you soon.
Doctor:	You will wait for us?
Man:	That is what I do, sometimes.

Exit Doctor to left of stage.

All is quiet. The Woman, Adam and Eve continue to sleep lying down as they were. The Advisor has drifted off to sleep too, sitting upright. The Man waits.

Enter Jester from right of stage, stumbling and stuttering.

Jester:	(*resting against the Advisor*) That is the last time I am made to be kind to those ungrateful, insufferable sods. (*notices that he is resting against the Advisor*) Goodness it's you! (*jumps away from him*) I mistook you for a rock! I'm sorry, I didn't mean to burden you! Why don't you move? Don't you hear me? Can't you? (*moves towards the Advisor and pokes him*) Are you…(*scared*)…dead? No, no, you can't be! It can't be! No! But…are you? (*checks to see if the Advisor is breathing*) You're still breathing. Thank heavens! Asleep then? (*pokes the Advisor again*) That must be it. Typical! (*moving towards the edge of the stage*) Everyone is, ultimately nonsensical. I'm sent off to fetch those fools only so that he, the exalted, can rest himself. I frantically searched for those blithering idiots, found them even though they couldn't be found, and so I returned, scathed and hurt, thinking how I'd stick it to them as soon as I see them. And why do I return? Only to find him shirking his duties, his sworn responsibility of deciphering whether he is he,

or him, and sleeping instead. That is why no progress is made. That is precisely why we are in this constant state of stagnated motion. Nothing happens, nobody comes, nobody goes, nobody wants, nobody needs. It's a death-trap, one from which there is no escape, at least until you reach the beyond. And that should be effortless, shouldn't it? After all, we all came to be with one foot firmly planted in our predetermined, undeniable, immovable destination. Even then, it is such an effort to reach that end. (*thoughtfully*) I wonder whether it is the same for he, or him. I suspect he must end as well. All things begin, and all things end, or have an end. Therefore, so must he. It is easy for someone like myself to think of such things. It is normal. (*returning to his train of thought*) No, he, or him, must have it easy. That's his reward for being identified as being special. Whose bright idea was it to decide that anyway? As far as I am concerned, I'm no different. (*laughing*) Hah! What fools we all are. It's amusing, really. Even self-proclaimed wise men like him (*pointing to the Advisor*) are nothing but incompetent, unfulfilled, incomplete beings. That is the hallmark of our kind. Soulless, treacherous, impure, unworthy. And so we look for meaning, we search for sense and significance, we hope for something new. We go to great lengths and depths, far and wide, to find it, to finally possess some substance. We never get there though, all our quests are ultimately in vain, doomed to fail. We remain hollow, devoid of meaning, substance, purity, devoid of purpose and being. (*laughs*) Truly amusing. (*laughs*) I wish I had an audience for my greatest joke, for this, my crowning glory. At least then my existence would serve a purpose. But it is not to be, for while one sleeps, the other two are nowhere to be found. (*pauses*) I am no different. I am just like the others, the rest. Meaningless, purposeless, incomplete, unfulfilled, impure. (*pauses*) I am a fool. (*distracted*) What was it again? (*looks around and sees the Advisor over his left shoulder*) Oh yes, I was sent away to find those two fornicators. (*goes up to the Advisor and pokes him*) Asleep. Well, then I too will sleep. I'll find a better place and lie down, just to show my contempt. (*looks around and moves towards the centre of the stage*) There has to be a comfortable patch somewhere amidst all this nonsense. (*sees the outline of more bodies lying down, those of the Woman, Adam and Eve*) What is this? (*alarmed, steps back towards the left of the stage and continues moving away, facing the bodies*) What have I here? Who are they? Where did they come from? Why are they here? Why wasn't I told? Why wasn't I consulted? What is all this? What fresh hell is this? Someone answer me!

Silence. All the commotion has woken the Advisor up. He stands up groggily, and tries to gather himself. He slowly starts to move towards the voices.

Man:	They are my companions.
Jester:	(*shocked by the voice coming from behind him, completely unprepared for it, jumps away and looks around*) Who speaks?
Man:	I do.
Jester:	(*still searching*) A man?
Man:	That would be me.
Jester:	Strangely familiar voice.
Man:	We have chanced upon one another in the past.
Jester:	(*squinting*) Who are you?
Man:	You know who I am sir.
Jester:	You know those people who lie there?
Man:	Yes, they are my companions.
Jester:	(*suspiciously*) What kind of companions?
Man:	The lady and I were married by the one that has metamorphosed. We then procreated, thereby producing the other two, a boy and a girl.
Jester:	(*unconvinced*) If what you say is true, then what are you doing here?
Man:	Do you wish to know what I am doing here, or what we are doing here?
Jester:	(*getting agitated*) What is a man, his wife, and their family doing in this desolate no man's land, in the middle of nowhere, away from their home?
Man:	Home is where the heart is. This is our home for the time being, till we journey on. Then this will cease to be our home. We hope not to have any more temporary homes on our way to our permanent residence, which is our destination.
Jester:	(*continuing to get agitated*) Your riddles don't amuse me. I'm beginning to find you intolerable.
Man:	I would not speak in riddles to a fool, a master craftsman such as yourself.
Jester:	(*taken aback*) How do you know that I am a fool?
Man:	I came to that conclusion the first time we met. Our subsequent meetings have confirmed that initial assertion.
Advisor:	(*reaching the Jester*) You know him too sir Jester.
Jester:	(*turning around to face the Advisor*) You are awake?
Advisor:	Yes, I am awake.
Jester:	When did you wake up?
Advisor:	It is too dark to tell.
Jester:	Were you awake all along?
Advisor:	Regrettably, I was not, contrary to my intentions.

Jester:	Who is he?
Advisor:	He is our new companion, the one we were led to by sir Knight. He is he.
Jester:	(*suddenly enraged*) I remember him now, I remember very well. (*facing the Man*) Preposterous pretender! (*drawing his knife*) Incongruous, inglorious heathen! I'll have your head! You will not escape this time! There will be justice!
Advisor:	Justice is not for you to decide, nor give.
Jester:	(*distracted, looking at the Advisor*) What do you mean?
Advisor:	You are a fool, it is not what you are meant to do.
Jester:	(*angry*) You can't know that for sure! Even if you know, I don't care! I am going to skin him alive!
Man:	You have an admirable weapon sir. It is long, with perfect aberrations.
Jester:	(*distracted*) Yes, she is pretty, isn't she?
Man:	It would be rude to disagree with the truth. You must be the envy of one and all.
Jester:	I would be if tales of its beauty were told far and wide. Modesty forbids me from doing so.
Man:	You are a good man. I shall speak of its legend if you wish me to.
Jester:	Would you be so kind?
Man:	If you so desire, nothing shall please me more.
Jester:	She is pretty, isn't she?
Man:	It would be rude to disagree with the truth. What does it do?
Jester:	What does what do?
Man:	Your weapon, what does it do?
Jester:	(*becoming angry all of a sudden*) What do you mean what does my weapon do? What is wrong with you? You are stupid and you make no efforts to make amends for it!
Man:	I apologise for not being able to satisfy you.
Advisor:	(*to the Man*) That is not your fault.
Jester:	(*calming down*) Yes, it isn't.
Man:	(*to the Advisor*) Would he still accept my apology?
Advisor:	Would you like him to?
Man:	I do not want any ill feelings between us.
Advisor:	But there are none! There could be none sir! You opened my eyes, there could be no ill feelings between us!
Man:	I am afraid I must correct you. It was he who awoke you, not I. As for the ill feelings, there are none, and, indeed, could never be any, between you and me. However, I sense there is some between myself and him.
Advisor:	You mean to say that you harbour ill-will against yourself?
Man:	No sir, there may be cause for concern between him (*pointing to the Jester*) and myself.

Jester:	(*to the Man*) Fear not, it's all in the past.
Advisor:	Are you sure?
Jester:	Of course I am! (*to the Advisor*) He is a fine gentleman, and he will speak of my legend wherever he goes. That is a very kind gesture. There could be no ill-will between two people who have such a relationship.
Man:	That is very kind of you.

Enter Doctor and Knight from left of stage.

Doctor:	Forgive us for taking so long. Are we late?
Knight:	Yes, we had to make every effort possible.
Doctor:	Yes, and it was only after we exhausted all possibilities that we decided to try again later and return. We didn't want to hold you up any longer.
Knight:	(*seeing the knife*) What is this? What is going on? What are you doing? (*jumping up and moving towards the Jester*) He is a friend… my friend. (*reaches the Jester. The two wrestle, the Knight easily overpowering the Jester and taking the knife off him and throwing him to the ground*) You can't!

The Woman and Adam wake up, startled by the loud noise. Adam sits up and looks around, the Woman stands up slowly and dusts herself. Eve continues to sleep.

Advisor:	They too are friends.
Jester:	(*to the Advisor*) Are we?
Advisor:	You decided all was well.
Jester:	(*getting up and dusting himself*) We are decided?
Man:	We have always been decided.
Advisor:	It is as he says.
Woman:	Sir Knight, you are back!
Knight:	(*seeing the Woman*) I am my lady, most humbly. (*bows and drops the knife*)
Woman:	(*walking up to the Knight*) And these must be your companions?
Advisor:	We are. (*picks the knife up and hands it to the Jester*)
Woman:	Are we to be introduced?
Knight:	Your wish is my command.
Jester:	(*takes the knife from the Advisor and sheathes it. He then notices the Woman*) You…you are…most…unusual.
Woman:	(*noticing the Jester*) Why, thank you! And that…(*sees the sheath and is very impressed*)…is a most impressive codpiece.
Jester:	(*smiling*) It is a sheath that conceals my trusted weapon.
Woman:	I am still very taken to it.

Knight:	(*clearing his throat*) If I may fulfil your command…
Woman:	(*looking at the Knight*) Mine?
Knight:	Yes.
Woman:	How rude of me to forget! Please sir, please continue.
Knight:	(*gesturing to the Advisor*) That is sir Advisor, and leader of our company. (*gesturing to the Jester*) That is sir Jester, though I suspect you have made his acquaintance. You and I have met before, of course, which leaves him (*pointing to the Doctor*) my friend, a recent addition to our party, but a dear friend.
Woman:	Delighted to meet you all!
Doctor:	(*to the Woman*) The pleasure is ours. (*to the Knight*) You didn't introduce her to our common friend.
Knight:	Who?
Advisor:	I think he means him.
Knight:	Who?
Jester:	(*growing impatient*) Him. (*point to the Man*)
Knight:	He is he, or him?
Doctor:	I don't know.
Jester:	What does it matter?
Knight:	Isn't that what he said?
Man:	I have not spoken lately.
Advisor:	Did I say that?
Knight:	Didn't you?
Jester:	It did sound like it.
Doctor:	Then we are decided?
Advisor:	We have always been decided.

Silence. Adam shakes Eve awake, and they get up. Eve leads Adam, and they exit to right of stage.

Silence. Jester moves closer to the Woman, and she welcomes his approach. They lose interest in everyone else, gets preoccupied with one another, and moves towards the centre of the stage, away from the others.

Doctor:	What now? (*looking at the Advisor, then at the Man, then back at the Advisor*) What now?
Advisor:	Are we all present?
Doctor:	(*looks around and counts*) Yes, we are.
Knight:	So what now?
Advisor:	We can continue our journey.
Doctor:	Our journey?
Knight:	Are you sure?
Advisor:	I am certain, if he is.

Man:	This journey that is being spoken of…
Advisor:	Yes?
Man:	Is it the same that I embarked on?
Advisor:	Yes.
Man:	The journey to the mental asylum on top of the hill?
Knight:	The quest.
Doctor:	The voyage.
Advisor:	Yes.
Man:	(*getting up*) Should that be the case, then I shall inform my companions of this fact. We can then continue.
Doctor:	Your companions?
Knight:	Are we not your companions?
Advisor:	Which fact?
Man:	Of course you are my companions, most kind sirs. However, I have a duty to my own, the ones I set out with originally. Since you already know and they do not, I feel it necessary to inform them so that they may prepare themselves. (*moving towards the centre of the stage where the Woman, Adam and Eve had previously been sleeping*)
Advisor:	Ah, that fact. Indeed.
Doctor:	That is a relief friend.
Knight:	(*panicking*) Speak not of relief! That cruel evil!
Advisor:	(*to the Man*) Is something the matter?
Man:	(*unable to locate Adam and Eve, ignoring the Woman and the Jester altogether*) Yes.
Advisor:	What is it?
Knight:	Speak up friend! I am here to help you.
Doctor:	We can collectively rectify any misdoings.
Knight:	And mishaps.
Advisor:	Indeed, but first we must know what it is.
Man:	I cannot find the boy and the girl.
Doctor:	I didn't see a boy and a girl, did you?
Knight:	Not recently, no.
Man:	(*to the Knight*) You saw them on our first meeting sir.
Knight:	I did?
Man:	Yes, though they did not interact with you. Children are wary of strangers, and their carefree characteristics do little to alter that.
Knight:	I did.
Advisor:	Is there a mother?
Doctor:	I am sure there is! Children out of wedlock are blasphemous! He wouldn't do such a thing, so fundamentally against what he stands for.
Advisor:	The mother could be deceased nonetheless.
Doctor:	(*ashamed*) Forgive me, I hadn't thought of that.
Knight:	(*to the Man*) Is the mother deceased?

Man:	No, she is not.
Advisor:	That is a stroke of good fortune. Where is she?
Doctor:	Yes, where is this mother? It falls on her to look after the children. Their well-being is her primary concern, her first priority.
Man:	She is around. You had met her earlier.
Advisor:	Do you mean the lady we met earlier?
Man:	Yes, the same.
Knight:	You are blessed sir.
Doctor:	Where is she now? Are you estranged?
Man:	It would appear so.
Doctor:	(*appalled*) Sacrilege! Twice erred, she treads on thin ice!
Advisor:	Tarry a while sir, your rebuke can wait. It is imperative that we find the children first.
Man:	(*pays attention to the Woman for the first time, but continues to ignore the Jester, who begins to slowly drift away from the Man and the Woman, towards right of stage*) I knew I would locate you. Do you know where the boy and girl are?
Advisor:	Who do you speak to sir?
Doctor:	Is it (*disgusted*) her?
Knight:	(*running across to the Man, who is now standing next to the Woman*) My lady, you are found!
Woman:	Was I lost?
Knight:	We misplaced you. I'll report to the others, they will come join us. (*runs back to the Advisor and the Doctor*)
Man:	(*to the Woman*) Where are the boy and the girl?
Woman:	(*looks on the ground where they stand*) Strange, they were right here! I'll look around. (*starts to look around the stage half-heartedly*)
Knight:	(*reaches the Advisor and the Doctor, catches his breath, then says to them*) She has been found!
Doctor:	The girl, or (*disgusted*) the other?
Knight:	Not the girl.
Advisor:	That is still good. She may know where the children are.
Knight:	I came here to fetch you.
Advisor:	Yes, let us go join them. We should all be together, it is for the best.
Doctor:	Must we?
Advisor:	Indeed, we must.
Doctor:	(*reluctantly*) Lead the way friend, we'll follow.
Knight:	It isn't very far. (*starts to walk towards the Man, the Advisor and the Doctor following. They stop many times along the way to allow the Knight to rest and catch his breath*)
Woman:	(*returning to the Man, looking alarmed and panicky*) I have looked everywhere, but I can't find them! (*turning away and shouting*) Adam! Eve! (*turning back to the Man*) It isn't any good! I can't find them!

Man:		When did you see them last?
Woman:		(*very worried*) When we woke up. I can't find them now!
Man:		They could not have gone very far. Calm yourself.
Woman:		(*panicking, almost hysterical*) It is all my fault! I can't find them! I am being punished!
Man:		Calm yourself. (*looking up*) Dawn approaches, but still no sign of rain. That is good, we may have some rain after all.
Woman:		(*worried and angry*) How can you think of such things now?
Man:		(*paying no attention to the Woman*) Rain…It did intrigue the boy. (*turning to the Woman*) Rain had intrigued the boy.
Woman:		(*worried and confused*) I don't understand.
Man:		It did not rain here.
Woman:		No, it didn't.
Man:		He is not here then. Therefore, he will not be found here.
Woman:		And the girl?
Man:		He is yet to master the art of seeing it feelingly. As such, I presume she has gone with him.
Woman:		Where are they now?
Man:		Not here.
Woman:		(*impatiently*) Then where?
Man:		(*pointing to the exit to left of stage*) Not in that direction, for we were there, and had they travelled in that direction, they would have passed us and we would have known.
Woman:		(*hesitantly pointing to the exit to right of stage*) Then in that direction?
Man:		It would appear so.
Woman:		We must go and look for them!
Man:		We must, but our party is incomplete.
Woman:		What does that have to do with anything?
Man:		We shall be misplaced by them if we leave without speaking to them.
Woman:		(*reluctantly resigning herself*) I see. Will they join us here?
Man:		Yes. (*looking over his shoulder*) And here they are.
Advisor:		(*walking up to the Man, the Knight and the Doctor following, with the Knight leaning on the Doctor*) Are we whole again?
Man:		No, we are not.
Doctor:		I am afraid his constant inability is beginning to pose a potent threat to his health. He begins to grow weary.
Knight:		(*bravely*) I'll be fine, don't worry. Where are the children?
Woman:		We haven't found them yet.
Man:		No, we have not, but we have deduced where they are.
Woman:		(*unsure, accusing*) He has deduced where they may be.
Advisor:		That is good news! Are we to go look for them?
Man:		Not all, that will slow us down.
Knight:		I'll go.

ACT 3 Scene 1

Doctor:	You can't, and neither can I.
Knight:	Why not?
Doctor:	Because you are in no position to form part of a search party. I can't go because someone has to take care of you.
Advisor:	Yes, and even if you did not have to take care of him, you still would not be able to go as you do not know what they look like. I cannot go for the same reason.
Woman:	That leaves just us.
Man:	(*distracted*) There is one other missing. Where is the fool?
Woman:	(*trying to change the subject*) Who? Oh look, it's getting late, and we still have a long way to go. We really must start looking for the children.
Man:	You do not know how far we have to go madam, you, like the rest of us, cannot.
Woman:	That's not true of all of us. The fool has been there before, he can tell.
Man:	Indeed, he did claim to have been there. That, however, was part of a conversation that he and I had in the absence of others.
Woman:	(*getting edgy*) Did you? Well, I may have over-heard. No, you must have mentioned it to me. That's it, that's how I know.
Man:	(*dismissing what the Woman said, turning to the others*) Where is the fool?
Advisor:	We did not pass him on our way here.
Jester:	(*from where he stands, at a distance from the others, on right of stage*) Hallo! Here I am! Are you all looking for me?
Advisor:	We have found you!
Jester:	(*walking up to the others*) You never lost me sir, I am your trusted servant.
Doctor:	(*looking suspiciously*) Where were you? Where did you go?
Jester:	I didn't go anywhere, I was here all the time!
Woman:	(*frantically*) Yes, yes, he was. I mean, no, he wasn't.
Jester:	Nonsense! I was! I heard about the children being misplaced, so I was looking for them.
Advisor:	You know what they look like?
Doctor:	No, he doesn't.
Knight:	(*distressed*) I am in pain.
Doctor:	(*to the Knight*) Courage friend, we will get to you.
Woman:	Yes, that's right, he was looking for the children, looking for Adam and Eve.
Man:	Did you locate them?
Jester:	No, I haven't been able to.
Man:	So you did not look where they are.
Jester:	(*getting angry*) If I knew where they are, they wouldn't be misplaced, would they?
Man:	You misunderstand me, but what you say is true.

Woman:	We must look for them. I'll go.
Man:	As shall I.
Woman:	No, you stay here, your wisdom will be needed here.
Man:	I fail to see how. Moreover, we are the only two who know what the boy and the girl look like.
Woman:	(*trying to remain composed*) Yes, well…I…well…you should stay here.
Advisor:	Is that your instinct talking?
Woman:	What? Oh, yes, yes, of course it is, it is my instinct.
Advisor:	Then you better remain with us sir, a woman's instinct should be trusted.
Man:	You know what you speak of, and so you must be believed. I shall do as you say and trust her instinct.
Jester:	(*casually*) Well, she can't go on her own, can she? She's a lady of respect, and it's still dark.
Woman:	(*earnestly*) And the landscape is unfamiliar to me.
Advisor:	We have already ruled ourselves out, there only remains you sir Jester.
Jester:	I was looking for the children earlier, I don't see why I can't look for them now.
Woman:	(*eagerly*) Yes, yes.
Advisor:	She cannot go alone, and you have previously done what she is now setting out to do. You are experienced, and she needs company. It follows logic that you go with her.
Woman:	(*eagerly*) Yes, yes.
Man:	We are set. Do not worry, you will find them as long as you follow my instructions.
Jester:	We're decided then?
Advisor:	We have always been decided.
Jester:	Very well, we're off. (*making for the exit to left of stage*)
Man:	Where are you going sir?
Jester:	To go look for the children of course.
Man:	Then I must correct your path. They went that way (*pointing to the exit to right of stage*)
Jester:	Yes, of course they did, of course they did. I was just…yes, very well, off we go. (*motioning to the Woman*) Come my lady.
Woman:	(*excited*) Oh yes, yes please!

Exit the Jester and the Woman, enthusiastically, to right of stage.

Doctor:	(*turning his attention to the Knight*) Now friend, what can we do for you?
Knight:	I don't know.
Advisor:	What is the matter?

Knight:	Is there a matter?
Doctor:	Of course there is! You are unwell.
Man:	He does not look it.
Knight:	That is true, I feel better.
Man:	Presently, perhaps, but if what your friend says is true of the past, then you must ensure that it does not happen again in the future.
Knight:	It's true. What do I do then?
Advisor:	You ought to rest, it did wonders for me even though I did not intend for it to happen.
Doctor:	Excellent suggestion!
Man:	(*examining the ground*) The land here lies fair. You will do well to rest here.
Doctor:	Yes, and we'll make merry here, so you won't be alone.
Knight:	I'll do as you say. But I thirst.
Advisor:	We all do, it epitomises your qualities.
Man:	It is never quenched for as long as we walk in these shadows, but our destination shall undo that curse and wash away the thirst.
Doctor:	(*setting the Knight down on the ground*) You're bleeding!
Knight:	(*pointing to his heart*) Here?
Doctor:	Yes.
Knight:	It is an old wound that has resurfaced. Don't worry, it signifies my improving health.
Advisor:	He speaks the truth.
Doctor:	Is there anything else we can do for you?
Knight:	No, thank you kind sirs, but I am fully armed, now that he has spoken.
Doctor:	Or him.
Knight:	Yes, that too.
Advisor:	You are well?
Knight:	I feel it.
Man:	Then you are.
Doctor:	Are you cold?
Knight:	No. (*falls asleep*)
Man:	Then he exists.
Advisor:	How so?
Man:	Are you cold?
Advisor:	No, but I do not understand.
Man:	Neither am I. None of us are cold, for it is not cold. Therefore, he exists.
Advisor:	I understand now. So he does.
Man:	Indeed.
Doctor:	Rest friend. (*gets up and stands with his back to the exit to left of stage*) You speak the truth, he is well.

Enter Adam and Eve from right of stage. Adam walks slowly, feeling around with his left hand. Eve holds his right hand and leads him. The Man and the Advisor are standing with their backs turned to Adam and Eve, and so do not notice their entrance.

Doctor:	(*looking over the Man's shoulder*) What's this? New players?
Advisor:	(*looking over his shoulder*) Or old ones returning?
Man:	(*turning around*) Neither, and yet some of both.
Doctor:	What do you mean?
Man:	That is the boy and the girl, and since we knew of their existence, they are not entirely new. Yet their tender age means that they are not old. They do play, however, as all children do, players of their own games, figments of their own imagination, strange creations that are lost with age, or forgotten.
Doctor:	(*goes to help Adam and Eve*) Don't be afraid little ones, you are amongst friends.
Adam:	(*lets go of Eve and feels around, then stumbles into the Doctor*) Who are you?
Doctor:	A friend.
Adam:	Or a foe?
Doctor:	No, a friend.
Adam:	Of whom?
Doctor:	Of you.
Adam:	But I don't know you.
Doctor:	The others do, and proclaim me as their friend. Well, most of them do anyway. It follows that I am your friend too.
Adam:	What about Eve?
Doctor:	The girl?
Adam:	I think so.
Doctor:	She is here, with you. You returned together, you holding her hand.
Adam:	Are you her friend too?
Doctor:	I am.
Adam:	Is father here?
Doctor:	I don't know, but one of the others may know.
Adam:	Can you take us to them?
Doctor:	Sure. (*takes Adam's hand and leads them to the Man and the Advisor*) We are here.
Adam:	(*letting go of the Doctor and feeling around*) Excuse me, but are any of you my father?
Advisor:	Hello young man, who are you?
Adam:	I am Adam.
Advisor:	That is a fine name.
Doctor:	He is looking for his father.
Man:	How are you boy?

Adam:	Father! It's good to hear your voice. Is Eve with us?
Man:	She is.
Advisor:	(*to the Man*) These are the younglings that we were so worried about?
Man:	They are.
Advisor:	The same ones whom two of our company set out for?
Man:	The same.
Advisor:	(*to Adam and Eve*) You have been located! Found! Rediscovered!
Doctor:	Great news!
Advisor:	(*to the Doctor*) Not yet friend, the two must return for this to be great news.
Doctor:	Forgive me, I was premature.
Advisor:	Happens to the best of us.
Knight:	(*suddenly sitting up*) If it does happen at all! Fortunate are you, even if you were premature friend! (*lies back down and goes back to sleep*)
Man:	(*to Adam*) Where did you go?
Adam:	I heard voices, mother spoke a little. Then I remembered about rain, and I went to go look for you to ask you about it. I explained to Eve which way to go, and then she led the way.
Man:	That is what I thought.
Doctor:	(*to the Man*) Are these children…yours?
Man:	Yes.
Doctor:	And the lady's?
Man:	Yes.
Doctor:	Are you two…together?
Man:	We once were, though, as you can see, we currently are not.
Doctor:	But when these children were born, you were…well…you were together?
Man:	Yes.
Doctor:	Wedded?
Man:	We were unified by said bond as you would have us.
Doctor:	(*relieved*) Fine children, fine children!
Advisor:	Yes, they are. (*to Adam*) Did you come across a fool?
Adam:	I wouldn't know one if I saw one sir.
Advisor:	(*to Eve*) What about you young lady?
Adam:	Please sir, she doesn't speak sir.
Doctor:	(*surprised*) Not a word?
Adam:	None sir.
Advisor:	(*to the Man, expecting a revelation*) She does not speak, and he does not see, does he?
Man:	He does.
Advisor:	(*Disappointed*) Does he indeed?
Man:	He sees it feelingly. However, he is yet to master the skill.
Advisor:	(*satisfied*) I understand now, they are pure.

Doctor:	Pure? I don't understand.
Advisor:	Untainted, straight from Sanctuary, pure.
Man:	That is correct.
Adam:	(*to the Man*) Where is mother?
Doctor:	She went looking for you with another of our company.
Adam:	I know that. I heard the rustle of some bushes, or leaves, and happy noises of two people. Eve led me to them. Right before we reached, mother spoke to us and told us to walk on ahead, to return here. She said they would walk behind us for our safety.
Man:	As would any careful, responsible lady.
Doctor:	(*snorting*) Bringing up the rear as it were.
Man:	(*to Adam*) It did not rain. Dawn approaches, and still no sign of rain. I am inclined to think that we may have some after all, before we reach there.
Adam:	(*looking hopeful*) Will we really father?
Man:	Patience boy, all will be well.
Adam:	Can Eve and I play?
Man:	Yes, you may. Stay near.
Advisor:	And don't disturb sir Knight.
Adam:	We won't sir. (*searching for Eve*) Come Eve, let's go play. (*Eve takes his hand and leads him to the right of stage, where they sit down and start to play*)

Enter the Woman and the Jester from right of stage.

Woman:	(*sees Adam and Eve*) Oh, you have arrived safely. Just as well, we thought we'd make sure.
Jester:	Yes, the two of us.
Woman:	(*walking towards the Man, the Advisor and the Doctor*) Yes…I mean…the two of us, yes, but separately.
Jester:	(*walking up behind her*) And together.
Woman:	But mostly individually.
Jester:	As well as together.
Doctor:	Are you two together?
Jester:	Yes.
Woman:	(*looking ashamed*) I…he is wise beyond measure, but this one has a fine weapon. I am so confused! I don't know! (*moves towards the back of stage and throws a hysterical fit, then sits down as if in a trance*) I am confused, I don't know.
Doctor:	I don't understand.
Jester:	We are together. We left together, we were there together, we returned together. We are together.
Doctor:	I understand that, but not what she says.

Jester:		It isn't easy for her, but she does what must be done. Needs must be met, though hard it may be.
Advisor:		She admires your weapon, but his wisdom.
Jester:		He can have his wisdom, we have made our peace and I'll stand by my word.
Doctor:		This doesn't seem right.
Knight:		(*suddenly sitting up*) Do what must be done, even if it seems wrong. It will feel right, sometimes right away, sometimes eventually. It will be right, for oneself and the other concerned, even if all others scorn. You will be relieved, so it won't matter to you. Who are they to scorn or judge? When it doesn't concern them? When it doesn't matter to them? It may matter to one other, perhaps two others, but there is nothing stopping you from conducting your own affairs, nothing. Abhorrent it may be, or worse, but I lay down my valour before you for it is not for me, or he, or him, to intervene. If he, or him, isn't to involve himself, who, then, is anyone else to do so? No, to each his own. Every man is in control of his own actions, dictated by none, altered for none. You take command and steer yourself to the destination, making your own road along the way. Do what must be done. (*lies back down and starts to snore*)
Doctor:		(*to the Advisor*) What is to be done?
Advisor:		Our company is whole, we can proceed.
Doctor:		(*pointing to the Woman and the Jester*) What about them?
Advisor:		They are part of the company, they travel with us. Though to where I know not.
Man:		(*walking to left of stage and sitting down facing the audience*) The destination remains unchanged, as has always been.
Doctor:		(*to the Man*) Are we all to be let in?
Man:		That is irrelevant as it has no bearing on the destination.
Doctor:		(*to the Advisor*) But…what about them? I mean, are they…do we…should they…
Advisor:		I can only answer that which is asked.
Jester:		Is he he, or him?
Woman:		(*remaining seated where she was*) Are we to travel now? To Sanctuary?
Doctor:		What?
Advisor:		I do not know.
Woman:		What do you mean?
Advisor:		I was not speaking to you madam, for your question has already been answered.
Woman:		That's a relief. (*to the Jester*) We are still on course. (*gets up and dusts herself*)
Jester:		Of course we are! Nothing can change that which is meant to be. Thirty pieces of silver is the same as two pieces of gold.

Doctor:	Nothing changes, nothing.
Jester:	(*to the Doctor*) Nothing changes nothing.
Doctor:	(*to the Jester*) But something changes something.
Jester:	(*to the Doctor*) Something changes everything.
Advisor:	Nothing changes, it all remains the same. There is no cause, there is no effect, no action, no reaction, no thought, no belief, no faith, no dawn. It has forever been so.
Doctor:	We are decided then?
Advisor:	We have always been decided.
Knight:	(*sits up, looks around, does not see the Man as his back is turned to him, turns around still seated, faces the Man*) Great news, we are all here! (*to the Man*) What are you doing?
Man:	(*looking at the audience*) I am waiting, that is what I do, sometimes.

Lights fade slowly as the curtain drops. End of Act and Play.

Epilogue

The Deliverance of Sanctuary
(from the book of poems titled *Cryptic Verses* by Ikhtisad Ahmed)

A man, a quest, a destiny, a place, no name, senseless sensibility.
Contradiction upon statement, bedlam unleashed amidst insanity,
Old questions resurfacing, new ones arising, persistence guaranteed;
No clear relation, yet woven together like muslin, together freed,
All of it coming together solely for that one true entity – sanctuary.
Man exists to give himself essence, life's quest to the place his destiny;
Seeking to establish what is yet unknown – be it liberation or delivery
That will come about for the nameless man and this mystical sanctuary?

No sense apparent because there is none to be made where none exists,
But that nagging feeling of there being hidden meanings about some
Greater thing, some larger purpose, some bigger picture, it persists.
The man's existence is his reason for readying himself for it to come,
Or perhaps for him to go to it through this state of perpetual stagnation?
Nothing ever changes in this no man's land, a figment of imagination,
That too of someone so perverse that he cannot see or decide about that
One hope for something, new or old, simply something, the deliverance.

It started in calm waters, and in calmer waters this sorrowful tale will end,
A fork in the road and only one path to choose for the hope to live on,
It concludes before the answer is seen or heard, the question unanswered,
An untimely end for the man, leaving each with conclusions to be drawn.

Lightning Source UK Ltd.
Milton Keynes UK
UKOW051125030412

190069UK00001B/64/P